FATED

USA TODAY BESTSELLING AUTHOR
SUSANA MOHEL

Cover Image by: Matty Gilbert

Editing by: Darlene & Athena @ Sisters Get Lit(erary) Author Services & Alexia Chase

Proofread by: Ari Basulto & Lucia ToMe

Published in the United States of America

NOTE FROM THE AUTHOR

This book contains elements of loss of a loved one, sexual

content, nudity,

medical issues, and racism.

Discretion is advised.

And the trouble is, if you don't risk anything, you risk more.

—Erica Jong

PLAYLIST

Free Fallin' – Tom Petty

Bent – Matchbox Twenty

Private Emotion – Ricky Martin ft. Meja

The Reason – Hoobastank

Bring Me to Life – Evanescense

Metallica – Nothing Else Maters

My Oasis – Sam Smith ft. Burma Boy

CHAPTER ONE

Elena

Kick ass.

Be awesome.

Repeat.

I've said the same speech a thousand times over the past few weeks. I know that my life could change with one misstep. In the distance, I spy the entrance to Freefall—the skydiving school that I've heard SO much about. Cautiously I wheel my trusty Ford 250 truck into the visitor parking spot and head inside, ready to empower myself from my crippling fear of heights. As I stride through the door, I feel ready for anything!

My outfit choice is inspired by comfort and quirkiness alike. Obviously I'm going to wear pants with no zippers—hello! What's even the point?—a sports bra and an extra-long gray t-shirt emblazoned with my family logo: *La Gloria*, The Glory—in Spanish, no less. With this as my armor, I'm ready to take on anything! After all, it's time to be absolutely awesome.

"Hi, how can I help you?" A blonde-haired girl behind the counter holding a clipboard asks me, I don't know who she is, but she doesn't look like a secretary.

"Hey, I'm Elena Posada. I made an appointment to jump today." The girl smiles in response, and her eyes light up.

"Hello, Elena, welcome to Freefall. My name is Brittany."

She holds her hand to greet me, and I'm eager to return the gesture. Her smile seems genuine, and I immediately take a liking to her.

"Is this your first time?" she asks. Surely she noticed my sweating palms after shaking my hand. Even though I have followed the instructions they gave me on the phone, I'm still shaking like a leaf.

"Is it that obvious?" I chuckle, but it sounds weird. It's clear my nerves are showing.

She doesn't say anything for a few moments, just smiles and looks at me with mild curiosity.

"Did you eat well? We don't recommend jumping on an empty stomach. If your glucose levels drop, you may feel dizzy, and the idea is for you to enjoy this."

If she only knew that before I left home, my father gave me his blessing and ensured my stomach was full. I normally eat a low-fat and low-carb diet, but I had a big bowl of fruit, yogurt, and granola.

"Here, I have your paperwork ready. There are some forms that you must sign before going to the teaching area, where you'll meet with one of our instructors who will give you the rundown for the jump."

Gee, this is getting serious. Am I going to regret this?

You only live once, I remind myself. That's why I am here. Because I want to live, do all those things that make me vibrate with adrenaline and make my heart beat faster.

Although mine doesn't beat like the others, mine is broken.

Brittany hands me another clipboard with some forms ready to be filled. The information is quite simple, my name, address, phone number, and below that, other important things like a waiver. The school guarantees to provide me with a licensed and trained instructor, along with a parachute in perfect condition. But other than that, by signing this, I acknowledge that skydiving is a dangerous activity.

How dangerous is skydiving?

According to the articles I have been reading in the past few days, during the last year, with more than two and a half million jumps, only thirty-five accidents have occurred. The risk is extremely low, but there remains the potential for death. Nevertheless, I am willing to do it.

I'd rather die on my own terms—living—rather than on a hospital bed suffering from a rare disease that no one can even pronounce the name of.

At the age of twenty-six, this is the first time I've tried something like this, and I'm not going to chicken out.

You only live once.

I sign at the bottom of the page and, with shaking hands, hand it to Brittany, who looks at me warmly.

"You can rest assured, you are in good hands. Although I am not in charge of the jumps, I can guarantee we have some of the best staff here. Emerson, the owner, has personally been in charge of training each and every one of them."

Sunny Hills wasn't the first place that popped into my mind when I thought of skydiving. Sacramento, the state capital, was the first keyword on the search engine, but then a Freefall ad appeared on my screen. After searching on Yelp and other specialized sites, I realized I didn't have to go any further. The answer was about twenty minutes from my orchard. This school has hundreds of five-star reviews and offers an excellent price for newbies like me.

Works for me.

So here we go.

After paying the fee and completing the paperwork, Brittany explains how to get to the training area. "Christopher will be waiting for you there. Also, you can leave your bag in one of the lockers. We'll take good care of you here." With that said, she winks at me and continues organizing something in the filing cabinet at the back of the hall.

That's my cue to stop delaying this.

Following Brittany's directions, I plod down the hall to the back toward the open door. The training area is so large that it is impossible to miss it.

"Hello, you must be Elena." A tall, burly guy with a shaved head waits for me there, smiling from ear to ear, and offers me a firm handshake. "I'm Chris. Welcome to Freefall. Lockers are over there. Ready to jump?"

"Well, no," I reply as a shaky smile appears on my lips.

"This is your first jump?" he asks me after I come back from leaving my handbag in the locker. To avoid carrying the key, they have implemented a fingerprint padlock, which is a nice touch.

"It's that obvious, huh?" I babble those words as I dry my hands on the fabric of my leggings.

"Mine too, so don't worry." God, I almost puke my heart out, he said it so seriously. For a second, I believed him.

Just for a moment, because he lets out a laugh throwing his head back. Mission accomplished because I'm also laughing like crazy, and my nerves are a thing of the past.

"Don't worry. Your priority should be having fun. Leave everything else in my hands. Emmy only hires the best staff, the same with the team. Everything here is top-notch."

The truth is, this information reassures me, and not only because he has repeated it like a parakeet would, but also because I have read the same thing in all the reviews from skydiving clubs and adventurers from all over the country who have come to this place. There must be a reason, right?

"We're going to fly to a height of twelve thousand feet," Chris begins to explain the technical details. "And we are going down at a speed of approximately one hundred and forty miles per hour."

This is the shot of adrenaline I've been looking for.

"Now, I need you to pay close attention to the directions I'm going to give you." He grabs a black harness that is on the counter at the end of the room.

There are straps and then more straps. With the mastery of someone who knows his business, he wraps each of the straps around my body. Suddenly, this starts to feel real.

I'm scared shitless. But fear won't stop me.

You only live once, I mutter to myself, repeating the mantra I've made my own over the past few weeks.

"Can I ask why you are doing this?" I must have nodded or something because Chris continues. "Did you lose a bet or something?"

I take a few seconds to think twice about my answer.

"The truth is that it's a challenge to myself."

He smiles as he tightens the last strap around my hip. "Those are the best. The competition with yourself. Good for you. Follow me. Let's move on to the next step."

I walk behind him to an iron structure with a platform lined with black rubber.

"This simulates the inside of the plane…" Chris begins, and I hasten to follow the instructions he's carefully giving. As if that weren't enough, there are some photos of each step at one end of the structure.

I'm so nervous that I pray that I can miraculously remember all of this once we are in the air.

"With these locks, I'm going to secure your harness to mine," he tells me, pulling the steel hooks on the sides of the straps. "They have a double-lock, so your security is well taken care of, as I said before…"

He pulls out a small cart with a flat surface that looks like a penguin cutout from somewhere.

Following the instructions, I drop down there, while he begins to explain to me what is going to happen once we are in the air.

I must hold on to the harness, stretch my arms, and lift my head so that my nostrils do not close up, preventing me from breathing. He continues with his instructions.

"We're going to free-fall for about thirty-five seconds, don't forget to keep your head up," he tells me, adjusting my position, and raising my calves. "We will turn from one side to the other, and then we will make two turns of three hundred and sixty degrees…" He moves the cart, making me spin on the floor like a rag doll.

At that moment, a garage door at the end of the room opens, and two men enter.

One of them is tall and thin, and the other seems to fill the space and consume everything. There is no other way to describe it. With the sun at his back, his shadow looms over me, enveloping me. I turn to see him. Those classic sunglasses hide his eyes, and a thick beard covers his chin.

From my precarious position, almost at ground level, he looks huge. And, of course, I had to be like this, with my mouth open and nearly drooling.

"We have another jumper today." Announces the guy who has come with him. Next to Mr. Hot Pants, Chris and the other guy look small. It could be from the way he walks, the confidence that comes from feeling comfortable in his own skin, or whatever, but the result is intoxicating.

I can't take my eyes off him. My gaze seems to have a will of its own.

As they approach, Chris stands to greet them.

"Cardan Malone," replies Mr. Hot Pants.

"By any chance, do you have something to do with the Malones here in Sunny Hills? The owner is married to one of them."

The man, Cardan, runs one of his large hands over his beard. *Sweet baby Jesus, how would you feel moving between my thighs?*

Calm down, wicked mind. I berate myself as I close my eyes, trying to stifle a groan.

"Hello, down there," he greets me, crouching down to be more or less at my height and raising his glasses. Rather so that his crotch is now at the level of my eyes—and *the* package he has there.

Lena, stop, now!

"And you are?" he asks me, looking at me with electrifying eyes the color of emeralds.

"Your jumping partner," Chris replies, and although I can't see him, I appreciate it. I doubt that at this point I can find my voice.

"Come," calls the other man, who I assume is the other instructor. "Let's start with this. The plane will be here in a bit."

They walk away, and I stare at the way those jeans fit, James Dean style. And the way he walks, moving his hips with a cadence and security. His entire body exudes power, owning it like he's walking on his territory after being handed it on a silver platter.

When he finishes with the instructions, Chris guides me to the same door that Cardan entered and then left. I follow him to some tables with umbrellas located at the foot of the track.

"You can have a drink or eat something while I go check the parachutes. We don't skimp on security measures here," he says before pointing to a bar with a girl behind it and walks away.

I'm not sure what to do. I'm neither hungry nor thirsty, as my stomach is in a tight knot. When I land, I'll reward myself with two shots of the one hundred percent agave tequila my aunt Maribel sent my father from Mexico. He only drinks it on special occasions.

A small white plane with a blue line across its width and a propeller on its nose comes out of a hangar. Suddenly, my pulse quickens. I follow it with my eyes as it begins its journey down the runway. It's not until I see it take flight that I let out a breath of air that I hadn't realized I was holding.

"Hey," says a hoarse voice from behind me, drawing my attention.

It's him again. Cardan.

"Good to see you standing," he smiles and extends his hand to greet me. He's already harnessed on, so I guess he's done with the theory part of this. The lines cross his body, his broad chest, his thighs. It is impossible for a man his size to fit in a harness the same size as mine.

Elena, don't look at his crotch, don't look... *shit,* too late.

I seem to have lost my voice, but I reciprocate the greeting with a smile.

"You never told me your name." He says, still smiling, his eyes are covered by the sunglasses. What a shame, because I would really like to see them again. "Cardan Malone, at your service."

"Elena Posada," I reply, though my voice comes out like a squeak.

Why doesn't the earth open up and swallow me whole? How many times am I going to embarrass myself today?

"Ready for the adventure of your life?" Oh God, he has no idea what this means to me.

"That's the question of the day," I answer and then add. "Well, for the first one."

The sun is quite strong, even if it is January and it is cold. In this part of California, we have been blessed with many sunny days. Which isn't only a delight to live in, but also makes it possible for my orchard to thrive the way it does.

Mangoes are a tropical fruit, after all. And although we are far from the tropics, we still manage to make it work.

Cardan looks at me with joyful curiosity, and I also reciprocate by looking into his eyes, little wrinkles are formed around them, which let me know two things.

First, this is a man who laughs often. The second is that he is a few years older than me.

And I'm dying to know how many.

"What's next after this?" he asks me, deciphering the meaning of my words. "Climbing Everest?"

He's much closer now, and his aroma envelops me, something earthly and masculine.

The heady mix is intoxicating. I could bury my face in his neck and memorize it for the rest of my life.

Oh, the things my overheated mind is conjuring up. I'm really missing a good fuck. I should add it to my list.

And speaking of that…

"That's at the end of my list, right after I find the pot of gold at the end of the rainbow and the Holy Grail, but first, I must get a tattoo and go swimming with sharks."

He opens his eyes before laughing again, confirming my theory. For me, there is nothing more attractive than a man with a great sense of humor.

Being interested in someone with an attitude like the green man who stole Christmas? No, that's not for me.

"Well, adventurous girl, you are going to need energy to achieve all that. Do you want to go grab a bite?"

No, no. I doubt that I can eat anything, this time for very different reasons. Now throwing myself out of a plane almost two miles above the ground and in free-fall seems very insignificant to me.

I want to know everything about him and whisper all my secrets in his ear.

But I'm not going to make it easy for him. If he wants something from me, he will have to prove it.

"Thanks, I had breakfast at home. I'm fine."

He puts a hand to the back of his neck, flexing his biceps, just barely contained by the sleeves of the gray Henley he's wearing.

This is better than porn. This is just for me and in live-action.

I put a hand to my mouth like I'm making sure I'm not soaking the floor with my drool.

"How about after landing, to celebrate?" he insists. His gaze doesn't leave mine for a second, as if he's searching deep into my brown eyes for the answers my mouth isn't uttering.

"We have to come back first, cowboy," I say with a wink.

He looks over my shoulder before adding, "And speaking of which, the time has come."

I turn around to see another plane approaching, it's longer than the first one I saw take off, but also narrower, and the line that crosses it is red. On the tail, it bears the school logo.

"The adventure is about to begin," Chris announces as he walks over to us. "Come, Elena."

I go to where he is, and he gives me the last tips before I follow him to the plane.

Cardan is already there. The same instructor with whom I saw him enter is securing him to his harness. Seconds later, I notice that without saying a word, Chris is doing the same.

I want to turn to talk to him, but this plane isn't pressurized, so nothing is heard beyond the wind's sound and the propeller in the front. Talking here is impossible.

The flight lasts about fifteen minutes, and when we reach the indicated height, my instructor opens the sliding door.

The moment is near.

"I'm going first," Cardan says loud enough for me to hear him above the noise of the wind.

"What about ladies first? Are there no longer gentlemen here?" I yell at him.

"Oh, chivalry will never go out of style," he defends himself. "The thing is, when you fall, I want to be there to catch you. See you on land. A celebration awaits us."

And without further delay, he and his instructor exit the plane into a free-fall.

"Ready?" Chris asks me loudly.

"We're next." Before I can regret it, I'm dangling my feet out of the plane, waiting for him to be the one to give the final pull.

There is no turning back.

My adventure has just begun.

Because you only live once.

CHAPTER TWO

Not having time to think about what's to come has a good and bad side.

The good. I haven't had much time to think about it—the jump—and maybe I would have regretted it.

The bad. I wasn't ready for the shot of adrenaline, and my heart feels like it's racing at a thousand beats per minute. This can't be healthy.

I'm screaming like crazy as I close my eyes for a moment while holding on tightly to the harness, just as Chris told me to do, until I feel his gentle pat on the arm. A signal I should open them and prepare to spin.

I thought this was going to be horrible, but the truth is, it almost feels like the air is a huge pillow supporting you. The feeling of dizziness I expected to devastate me never comes, but instead, I'm enjoying the moment.

It is so different from anything else, and I love it. Despite the icy wind scraping my cheeks, it's loud and exciting. Really exciting.

"Raise your head," I hear Chris yell in my ear.

I do what he tells me, and I take a much-needed deep breath.

Another tap on the arm, and I grab onto the harness, feeling the pull of the parachute opening and lifting us up. This must also be what those who jump off a bridge experience.

I feel the air pockets and crosswind currents.

Without a doubt, this is the craziest thing I have ever done in my entire life.

I'm kicking ass, for sure!

We've slowed down. I stay in silence for a moment enjoying the strange sensation that invades my chest. I'm sure it's because of the adrenaline—what a powerful drug. This is a unique opportunity to observe the world from a new perspective. One not many tend to experience.

I swear I can see the neatly uniform tree rows of the orchards in the distance.

And it's wonderful.

God, I'm flying.

Falling down.

Chris places my hands on the parachute cords to direct it and look where I want to go.

I'm glad he has a camera in his hand because I want to be able to watch this over and over again.

In the distance, I see Cardan with his instructor. They are much lower than us. *Now isn't the time to think about him. Enjoy this, Lena.*

I raise my eyes again. It's true what they say, time flies when you're having fun. Sooner than I expect, we'll be on land, and this experience will be over.

Although I told Cardan that the next thing would be a tattoo, the truth is I haven't decided yet what my next step will be. All I can think about is him—Cardan—the man I just met and now can't get out of my head.

Dammit.

Chris's hands rest on mine as he points to a large green area in the distance, next to a roof decked out with the Freefall logo. Up ahead is our landing zone. The adventure is coming to an end.

And I'll treasure this memory for a lifetime, even if it might be shorter than most. It doesn't matter.

With the ground only a few feet away, I lift my legs as instructed and gently touch the ground. What Chris said is true. They hire people with a lot of experience. We land smoothly, without any incidents. I imagined this would be bumpier, considering we fell from several miles high.

"Give me a moment to unhook you," Chris says, flipping the latches, letting me go.

My legs are shaking. I'm only standing by pure miracle. My bones have turned to jelly, and blood runs furiously through my veins as my heart threatens to leap from my chest.

Calm down, I scold myself. We're not in the mood to have a heart attack today.

"What did you think about it?" Chris asks me after giving me a few seconds to compose myself.

"One of the best experiences I have ever had. Thank you very much."

He gives me one of those quick hugs and begins to pick up the parachute after pointing out the school and the cafeteria. I definitely need something hot to drink and to catch my breath before driving back to the orchard.

I think about what lies ahead for me today; life in the countryside is calm, but it also means I've several tasks that I must fulfill.

We are preparing for springtime, which means that we are fertilizing the ground. Mango trees are wonderful. They take a lifetime to grow, which guarantees us a production of at least twenty years. A few months ago, we bought another plot of land in the northern part of the orchard, and we've started planting new trees. Even though I'm the youngest of five siblings, my older brothers never intended to take over when my father retired—but I always liked it. They took the money my father gave them to start their lives elsewhere, and although we are still quite close in *La Gloria,* only the two of us remain.

My mother sadly passed away at the beginning of the year, just a few weeks ago.

And then we took another blow.

As I take a few steps, I realize that Cardan is there, with his hands in his pants pockets, waiting for me with a smile gracing his face.

"Did you enjoy it?" he asks me. In response, I give him a smile from ear to ear.

"More than I expected." And that's the plain truth.

"Now, you're getting the tattoo, right?"

I was joking before, but I think I'm going to do it. Never mind, I don't think so. I'd have to find something meaningful that I want to brand on my skin forever.

"And swimming with sharks, don't forget about that," I remind him.

"Any chance you'll accept my invitation for a drink first?"

I look him over from head to toe. The man is exceptionally sexy, and, from the way he behaves, surely he is used to getting away with things often. Well, not with me—that'll take a bit more work, and Cardan Malone has yet to find out how much.

"I'm going for a drink. It's up to you if you want to join me." Although I want to keep my eyes glued to his face and discover more about him, I turn and walk to the outdoor cafeteria without looking back.

My heart continues to beat furiously, this time, the shot of adrenaline coming from a different source.

Be awesome.

I'm positive he's the one following me after a few minutes. *He is,* I know it's him because, after a few steps, I see him walking by my side out of the corner of my eye.

The small café doesn't offer alcoholic beverages, so I just order a Chai tea to kill the cold, and Cardan orders a black coffee.

"So, Elena, do you come here often?"

How else can I answer that cheesy line than by laughing out loud? From the expression on his face, I can tell that that was his mission in saying it.

Mission accomplished.

"That's the worst line of all," I tell him as I blow on my cup of tea to cool it down before I take my first sip.

"And you're the most elusive girl I've ever met," he chides me. "Why is it so hard for you to give me a simple answer?"

He takes off his sunglasses. Damn, I'm glad we're sitting. Otherwise, my knees would be so weak they would fail me. Those green eyes do things to me.

"What do you want?"

He smiles and looks me in the eye again. "There you go again. Answering a question with another question. But here, I'll answer, what do I want? To get to know you better."

And before I dive into the deep end with him, I need answers.

"If you are looking for easy prey, you're wasting your time. I'm not your girl."

He opens his eyes, surprised by my words, and frowns. After a few seconds, he responds, "What makes you think that's what I'm looking for, Elena, we're just talking. Sorry, my intentions weren't to make you uncomfortable."

My Latin blood boils. If I have anything running through my veins at this moment, it is undoubtedly fire.

"How old are you, Cardan? A man like you surely has a wife and kids waiting at home. Take the band out of your pocket and put it on. Man-up and stop flirting with me."

He stares at me like I've slapped him.

"Now, I'm offended," he begins to speak. "If I were married, believe me, she would be here with me. Sharing this adventure together. If she were afraid of heights, I'd have brought her simply because I couldn't be far from her. My wife would surely be on the ground, recording this experience with her phone to show it to our friends and to laugh at me. If I had decided to marry someone, I would be committed mind, body, and soul to her. And I certainly wouldn't be here with you, flirting as you've said. I'm thirty-eight years old and too old to play games with someone else."

He may have been the one that released a string of words, but it's I who was left breathless. The way he spoke, so sure, without any hesitation. Those piercing green eyes, staring into mine.

Now what do I say?

Boom.

Boom.

Boom.

My heart beats fast and hard.

"I have a mango orchard near Sunny Hills. I've lived in this area my whole life, and until a few weeks ago, I didn't think the world was worth leaving my bubble, but now I want to see it all."

Not only does that seem to satisfy him, but his eyes sparkle with curiosity, I mentally buckle up, preparing myself for the questions to come.

But once again, it is he who surprises me.

"I understand what you're saying." There he goes, again stealing my breath without even touching me.

Why is his presence so powerful?

Why do I feel something pulling between us, like gravity?

"I have visited a lot of places, seen many wonders. Got lost in beautiful cities and witnessed sunsets in many places, but it's useless when you don't have someone to share it with."

I take another sip from my cup while I think about his response. The tea is at the temperature I like, neither too cold nor too hot. Tepid, just like my life, and that's why I decided to turn my destiny around.

"Don't they call what you've described a midlife crisis?" I can't help my daring response. I've always had little filter when speaking. Sometimes I think the wire that connects my mouth to my brain has a short circuit.

He laughs again. I love the sound, hoarse and deep. I love even those little wrinkles around his eyes and how his wide chest moves.

I want to touch him, to feel his bare skin and his muscles moving under my fingers.

"I don't know," he answers sincerely. It shows in the tone of his voice. "The truth is, I've decided to find a good place to settle down, cast my luck, and Sunny Hills seems like the right place. There is something inviting about it."

That is true. Although I have never lived in town, the area is very nice, the people are friendly and welcoming to newcomers.

This is a small town full of people with big hearts.

"You'll enjoy it here."

"Then why do you want to leave?"

"Because life is a bitch sometimes." My answer is vague but full of truth.

We look into each other's eyes, the moment is intense, and neither of us wants to spoil it with words. After a couple of minutes I go back to my cup, watching a group of college students, all dressed in UC Davis hoodies, get on a plane with the instructors. We wave at them, wishing them good luck.

"I'm starving," Cardan breaks the silence. "How about you show me your favorite place to eat?"

I know the perfect place.

After collecting our things from the locker, we go out to the parking lot.

"This is mine," I tell him, pointing to my truck.

"I'm right next door," he replies.

And as I turned to climb into the driver's seat, a new fit of laughter bubbles up in my chest.

This couldn't be more cliché.

"What?" he asks me, looking offended.

"You're definitely in the middle of a crisis," I reply, pointing to his car. "Nothing is more obvious that a man is trying to make up for something than a sports car."

We both focus our attention on the car, my eyes scanning it from the hood to the bumper. The truth is that it is beautifully restored and obviously vintage.

"This is a '68 Mustang GTA, and I've been driving it for over ten years or so. I don't think it's a symbol of the crisis that you say I'm experiencing."

A smile tugs at his lips, and mine do the same.

"Are we going to eat or what?" I say after a short beat of silence.

"Lead the way."

And he has no idea how good it feels to hear him say that.

♡♡♡

I drive my truck carefully to Lulu's Diner, the place is an institution here in Sunny Hills, and those who are looking for something delicious without much hassle don't hesitate to come here.

The restaurant is empty when we arrive as we get here before the lunch rush, so Cardan and I smoothly settle into a booth in a corner.

He sits across from me, both of us beside the window. And, even if I wish he had sat next to me, with one of those strong arms around me, I know it's too early for that.

This isn't even our first date.

Or is it?

No, it can't be. This is a casual outing, two strangers who met in the middle of an adventure and decided to fulfill a basic function. Eat.

"What's good here?" he asks me as he settles against the vinyl cushion with the comfort of someone who has done this many times.

"Everything!"

The waitress comes to serve us coffee, and we both order. I decide on half a sandwich and a cup of chowder, after flying—or, rather falling—something hot would make me feel good. Sadly, it's not the hot man sitting in front of me.

"So," Cardan says after taking a small drink from his cup of black coffee. "The next stop is San Diego?"

My brow furrows, I have no idea what he means.

"Why would I go to San Diego?"

He smiles while looking at me indulgently.

"Didn't you say the next thing is to swim with sharks? For that, we have to go a little further south."

We? As in *us?*

"And since when are you invited?"

"Today, I decided to accompany you." He answers with a smile.

"I haven't decided anything," I exclaim.

"San Diego is several hours from here, you could easily take a road trip down, but it's going to be better with someone—me—to take over the wheel after a few hours," he begins. "Or you could take a plane. I know you're not scared, but I can still be useful there, you know, to hold your hand during the landing."

That makes me laugh, but hey, it's time to tell the truth.

"The truth is, I still haven't decided on my next adventure. It might take a while before I can do it. You see, currently, we are fertilizing and also planting new trees in the orchard on a new piece of land we bought that overlooks a small creek. I'm pretty busy."

He looks at me, considering what to say next.

"You manage an orchard by yourself?" He raises his eyebrows at those words, clearly surprised. It is not common in this area for a young girl to be in charge of an orchard, but hey, my brothers built their lives far away, and I am the only one left at home with my father.

"My mother passed away a few weeks ago. My father has not been the same since."

Neither am I, but I don't want to ruin the moment by talking about something so depressing.

"Is it just the two of you?"

"In a way, yes," I reply before telling him about my brothers. I'm not lying when I mention how proud of them I am and the fact that they were strong enough to choose their own path without looking back.

Although it left me without many options.

"And what do you want?" he asks me, looking into my eyes. It may be a seemingly simple question, but to answer, I need to think carefully.

There are many angles I must consider. And so little time to do it.

"I like life in the orchard," I say, taking a sip of my coffee. "About a year and a half ago, I started a project to dehydrate the mangoes and add chili to them as a snack."

"Mango with chili?" He seems interested, really interested.

"Yes, my parents are Latino. My father came from Mexico for work when he was very young, and my mother was born here, although my grandparents were also Mexican. They met because my father worked in the orchard and well, the rest is history."

"Do you speak Spanish?" This conversation goes from one place to another, and I love it, I feel that I am sharing my story with him without it being heavy.

"Fluidamente," I reply, I have some accent, but I can express myself comfortably in Spanish.

"Knowing a second language is smart. I bet it helps you with your workers or when communicating with your family on the other side of the border."

"Very much," I agree. "At home, we always speak Spanish to each other. My parents were determined that we know the language. One of my brothers, who works in sales, says the same thing."

"So, about your mangoes with chili, tell me more."

The waitress brings the food, and between bites and spoonfuls of the thick, delicious soup, I explain my plan.

"A few months ago, I bought my first dehydrator. But then, with my mother passing, life has been a bit too hectic since then."

And I lost the ability to make plans. I'm living a day at a time.

He looks at me. His green eyes have softened, but the intensity is still there.

And those arms, how good they would feel around my body, comforting me, pressing me to his chest with force.

It's time to change the subject.

"What about you? What brought you to the area?"

"Work," he says after swallowing. "I was also looking for a change, the pace of the city can be exhausting at times, and clearly, I'm no longer a spring chicken."

"San Francisco?" I love that city, its spirit, the architecture. The food and culture.

Not to mention that it is by the sea and the weather is wonderful.

"Worse," he laughs. "Los Angeles, I had to run before I choked, and not just because of the smog."

Now I'm the one who laughs.

"A stalker chasing your steps?"

He runs a hand through his beard before answering. "No," and upon hearing it, I raise my eyebrows, curious to know what he's going to come up with next. "My mother wants grandchildren, and I am her only child."

"And you want children?"

"Isn't it too early to discuss children? Shouldn't you wait until at least the third date?"

I laugh out loud, and he does the same.

Practicing with him would be very entertaining *and* exciting for any woman. Too bad, I'm not the right woman.

"The truth is that yes, not right now or next month either. But it is something I would love."

He's figured it out because after that, he changes the subject to something lighter, the latest Marvel movie and our theories of what's to come.

Of course, when the bill arrives, he insists on paying.

"My mother brought me up well. No gentleman lets the girl pay on the first date or any to follow."

"Good to know that you are a feminist, Malone."

"To the core," he answers. "But chivalry will never go out of style."

We leave the restaurant when the place starts to fill up, and we walk very close together to where we park our cars.

"When can I see you again?" he asks me, leaning his arm to the side of my head, trapping me between my truck and his strong body. He's so close that I can feel his warmth, and I want to melt into him.

Make him mine.

"I don't know," I reply, biting my lip to stop my smile.

Leaning my hands on his chest, I push him gently, although what I want is to wrap my arms around his neck and kiss him until my lips numb.

He lets himself be carried away, his arm falling to the side of his chest, but his eyes are still fixed on mine. Looking for an answer.

"What do you think if we leave it to fate? If it is written in the stars, we will meet again."

My answer leaves him paralyzed for a moment, so I take advantage of his distraction to get into my truck.

Fate.

Bad idea to leave it in its hands. Because life is a bitch.

CHAPTER THREE

As I drive to the orchard, I can't stop thinking about Cardan. He came to town searching for a future. A place to settle down. He wants to have children, the normal thing. Most people dream of a family, of putting down roots.

I'm a girl who has no future, who must limit herself to living day to day. That's why I insist on living life to the fullest.

No restrictions.

No regrets.

Well, I don't have that much freedom, to be honest. My father depends on me a great deal now that I am running the orchard.

Being in my shoes isn't easy, but I refuse to play the victim.

You only live once, and I'm willing to make the most of my last breath, but I also have responsibilities that take precedence.

I contradict myself so much that even I'm confused. Maybe I should talk to a professional to help me sort out my mess.

I park my truck in the usual place. When I enter the house, I find my father in the kitchen, sitting at the table, looking at the orchard through the large window.

"You came back," is the first thing he says to me. I think he's relieved.

"What? Did you think you were going to get rid of me so easily?"

My father smiles, but there is no joy in his eyes; it disappeared with my mom.

"I have a video if you want to watch it."

He shakes his head in response. "I know tomorrow is Sunday, but Alexander wants us to go see how the new trees are doing. I thought you and I could go for a walk in the canyon and maybe have lunch there."

Wow, he wants to go out? This is a first. Since we returned from the cemetery, my father hasn't left the property, not even once.

Maybe it's a trap—to talk to me in a neutral place. But after everything we've been through lately, I'm willing to take the risk.

"Sounds like I have a date with the main man in my life," I reply, smiling at him.

His dark eyes light up for a moment, but the excitement fades as fast as a lit match.

"I hope one day you meet the love of your life. A man who sweeps you off your feet and makes you fall madly in love."

I look at him, narrowing my eyes.

"And what happened to the jealous father thing, *papá?* Aren't you supposed to say no man is good enough for your daughter?"

His gaze becomes cloudy again. I feel the same as him. We both know why.

"What all parents want for their children is to see them happy. Building lives on their own and reaching their goals."

I take a long breath before answering.

"That's why I went to jump off the plane today because I want to live."

I'm going to die living to the fullest.

He looks at me, his eyes filled with the wisdom of someone who has lived many years. And he has learned countless life lessons.

"That isn't living, *niña.* That feeling is instant that only lasts for a second, and then what are you left with?"

"I have the memories." I look back at him and try to act as confident as possible, but to no avail. My father knows me well.

"You're too young to live just on that itself," he says before getting up to walk down the hall.

He will surely spend the rest of the afternoon locked in his study, consumed by his own memories.

Looking for something to entertain myself, I search the closet on the first floor for my jacket, change my sneakers to my work boots, and head to the orchard.

Better to see how things are going instead of staying home thinking about the guy I met today. No, he's not simply just a guy. The word is too small for him. Cardan Malone is all man.

I walk among the orderly rows of my beloved trees. If they could speak, oh, the stories they would tell. I grew up running between them with my brothers, playing hide-and-seek, seeking shelter among the branches when it was hot, or picking unripe fruits to eat secretly with chili powder.

We were free here. We grew up without fear because we were safe in our home.

What we didn't know is that the enemy often doesn't attack us from outside but hides in the silent refuge inside us.

There, where no one can hear it.

And when you least expect it, it hunts you down.

The soil around the roots has been carefully removed for compost. Although mango is a tropical fruit, my grandfather developed a very clever—and efficient—way of adapting it to the terrain and climate of the Northern California valley. First, trying various grafts, learning from trial and error, after that, they found the perfect mix of nutrients and the technique to stimulate growth annually.

Today, many years later, we continue to expand our business, honoring the family tradition. We, the Posadas, are tied to this land in the same way that these trees have put down their roots here.

The sun is fading over the horizon when I come home. I'm exhausted, hoping that helps me to fall asleep quickly. Lately, I've been working to exhaustion because it's hard for me to fall asleep. I've researched various techniques online for insomnia; some suggested creating a routine, and so on. Although I've followed the advice, there are still some nights where I spend hours staring at the ceiling before I finally surrender to the sands of sleep.

Tonight is no exception, even though I've taken a hot bath to relax. Sleep still evades me, but it feels different this time. Because of him, my body feels like it was hit by lightning.

I want to feel his strong body moving over mine, between my legs, as that husky voice speaks into my ear, telling me what he's going to do next.

There's only one word to describe this—horny—but, I'm sure the battery-powered boyfriend hiding in my nightstand drawer is going to do very little to satisfy me.

After tossing and turning in bed, I finally fall into a restless sleep. He's still there in my dreams, with his green eyes looking at me with intensity as his fingers run over my hot skin, going down the valley between my breasts, drawing a road map across my belly to then getting lost between my legs.

I wake up agitated and upset. I'm sweating despite the cold this time of year. Damn that man. Who does he think he is to torment me in this way?

He should wear a shirt with a warning stating dangerous goods, highly addictive man. Or maybe what I should do is find someone to have a good time with and make Cardan Malone something of the past.

Blame it on the drought I'm going through.

Keep telling yourself that, Lena, the voice in my head yells at me, but I decide to ignore it. I think it's better if I get up and take a shower to cool me off. My father told me Alexander, the man we hired, is coming to speak with us, and knowing my father, I'm sure he meant at seven in the morning.

Here in the orchard, it doesn't matter that others think it is a day of rest; life in the countryside never stops.

There is not a single dull day, despite what many people may assume.

♡♡♡

"Dax wants to talk to you," my father tells me once we are sitting at a picnic table in one of the recreational areas.

Although it is Sunday, there are very few people around, it's relatively quiet. In the summer, it is very different. We wouldn't have even found a spot in the park.

"You know what I think about it." Dax Pearson is the doctor who works at Sunny Hills General, our local hospital. And no, this has nothing to do with romance.

My father didn't even let me take a bite of my *machaca* burrito before ambushing me. I was expecting something like this. My father has made it extremely clear what he thinks about my situation, and what he expects of me.

But this is my life, and I want to have control over it, and no one else gets a say. At least as much as possible.

Or have I gone nuts?

He looks at me the way only a father can. Even though I'm already a woman, I suddenly feel like a little girl who has been caught red-handed and has no way of denying it.

Nor to flee from the consequences.

"What a way to ruin lunch, *papá*," I reply as I drop the burrito on the waxed paper, I wrapped it in. The shredded meat, potatoes, and the sauce my mother taught us all to make when we were teenagers—so delicious—but gone to waste.

He stares at me again.

"I'm worried about you, Elena," he tells me.

I know. I don't want to be the one who puts more weight on my father's shoulders, but he doesn't understand that if he relaxes and lets go of all this, he'd be better off.

"Maybe it's time we both got a therapist," I say, mulling over the subject. "You need to deal with the grief and responsibility you think you have over me. And I need to learn to accept my destiny."

My father hasn't even unwrapped his burrito. He's more concerned about me than satiating his hunger.

"You know there are options, *niña*. This isn't a death sentence. But a yellow light."

"A yellow light that at some point will change to red, and I refuse to live in fear. It's not what I want for myself."

He stares at the water a few feet from us, his eyes on the horizon for a couple of minutes. The cold air envelops us.

"I'm not asking you to live in fear, just to be aware that you are…"

I know what he's going to say, and that infuriates me.

Boom.

Boom.

Boom.

My heart beats furiously, like the fire that runs through my veins. "I'm more than that. I refuse to let it define me. I *am* Elena Posada."

He thinks carefully about his words before answering. "Of course you are, but you also inherited…"

Yes, I *inherited* my mother's character. While my father is a quiet man, my mother was a firecracker, just like me. That's the legacy that defines me.

That's what my genes say.

"We'd better go home. I have some laundry to do." It's a good excuse, even though it's just the two of us; with the amount of clothes in the basket, it seems that we change at least six times a day, along with my brothers sending over their things to be taken care of.

My father and I do not exchange a word as we return home. We barely glance at each other. Upon arrival, he takes refuge in the study, and I keep myself busy with the laundry. It really wasn't just an excuse.

The pale-yellow walls of my room suddenly feel like they're closing in on me, I need to breathe. I need a drink and a good fuck. But since my options are limited, I do the next best thing.

I pick up the phone and dial the number for Destinee, my best friend. No one in the world understands me better than her.

"I'm mad at you for going skydiving without me, but please tell me all the juicy details. Don't you forget who you're talking to, girlie. We grew up together, remember? You can't hide anything from me," she exclaims as soon as she saw me.

I burst into laughter. "Dee, come on, I know you're not really mad."

"Just tell me already! Was the instructor hot? Did you meet any eye candy out there? What did you do? Spit it out!"

Should I lie or be honest with her? I can never seem to keep anything from my best friend—we practically grew up together, and she's like a sister to me. Two younger sisters and six older brothers meant there was no hiding anything from Dee.

"Well...ahem," I started. "I guess you could say that I met someone out there."

The room fell silent; she was holding her breath in anticipation.

"Spill it! Everything!"

And so, I told her the story of how I met him, his handsome face, and even his last name: Malone. Of course, we both knew who the Malones were—the heartthrobs of Sunny Hills that had made headlines once they found their other halves all those years ago. Despite settling down and having families of their own now, they were still very active members of the community. In such a small town like ours, everyone knew everyone.

"A new *single* Malone in town, how exciting. They are so freaking hawt!"

"I don't know if they are related. I didn't ask him much. Actually, he was more interested in knowing my story than in telling his own."

"Too bad," my friend sighs.

"But... now, that you bring that up, I can recall Chris, my instructor, did ask him, and he replied that he has no idea."

But now that I think about it, I also want to know his story.

"When you see him again, you have to take control of the conversation, Lena, make him spill the beans."

When I see him again—I would like to know when that day is going to happen. It'll truly be a miracle, especially with him mentioning fate.

"I don't understand how you could be so stupid. Why didn't you at least give him your phone number?" She scolds me. "Damn, I would have kissed him right there in the parking lot."

"Shouldn't you be setting a good example for your sisters?" I say, laughing. Destinee has some wild ideas when it comes to men. Despite that, she is the best friend a girl could have in the whole wide world. Without her and her family's support, I wouldn't have survived after my mother died. I was so lost.

"Desirae and Devynn are fine, still playing with dolls. By the time they're teenagers, I'll be happily married to my oil tycoon."

"Last week, he was a famous Hollywood actor. I wonder what he'll be next week."

"That's not important, as long as he's well endowed, and I'm talking about both his bank account and…"

"You're crazy…" I laugh at her overexuberant nature.

"Hey, it's possible. Anyone can have their own Anastasia miracle. I'm saving myself for my very own version of Mr. Grey."

"You aren't saving yourself for anyone, liar." I laugh again. Dee has a pretty active social life, and she never lacks a male companion. Of course not. She's a beautiful girl with a heart of gold.

I wish my brother David hadn't been such an idiot. If he wasn't, then I would be calling her my sister instead of just my friend. But that's a story for another day.

"I'm guarding my heart, but my body is learning everything it needs to know." Unlike me, my friend went to college in Davis, a reasonably close city. But now she has moved back to town to live alone, where I have always been since I attended the local school.

"My father told me today I should speak to Dax Pearson." Dee is a nurse at Sunny Hills General, so she knows exactly who I mean.

"Lena, you know what I think about it," her tone of voice has changed. No more jokes. This means she's serious.

Another sigh comes out of my mouth. "Please don't be Nurse Jensen with me; just be my friend."

"I have and will always be your friend, Elena Maria. But I also need to be honest with you, and I think you are wasting valuable time. You're risking…"

No, no, not this conversation again. I've already made up my mind about it.

"My father is calling me," I lie. "I gotta go."

"Don't you dare…" I hear her say, but I've already pressed the red button on my cell phone screen.

No, I can't go back to the same thing. What I need is to find a way to take control of my life—to keep it. I'll live by my own rules. Mine. Only mine.

Because you only live once.

After another sleepless night, dawn breaks, and duty calls. On Mondays, there are more than enough things to do. I need to go to the bank to sign some papers, then to the general store to pick up some stuff I ordered a few days ago, and maybe go to Sunny's Café for breakfast. They serve the best pancakes in the county.

I dress in tight jeans, a long sweater, and brown knee-high boots. I fix my hair and even put on some make-up, which I don't usually do, unless I'm going into town.

It doesn't take more than an hour at the bank. When I leave, I realize that my truck's right front tire is almost on the ground, and I don't have a spare. Wonderful. Without wasting any time, as I still have a lot to do, I call the tow truck and ask them to take me to the nearest garage.

The trip to the garage is quite short, and I was surprised. I thought this place was closed. They have completely remodeled it, making it look top-of-the-line. Everything is modern, clean, and clearly new.

I open the office door, the hot air hits me, and there's a surprise in here for me, too. The surprise is hearing the voice I have been dreaming about for the past two nights.

"Wow, it seems fate is on my side."

Damn, isn't that the truth?

"Are you stalking me?" I ask him when I can finally catch my breath.

"Since this is my business, I think it is rather the opposite."

I want to give him a clever answer, to call him a liar. But because of his work shirt with his name embroidered on the left pocket, he leaves me little opportunity to do so.

"Blame it on fate," he says as he walks over to me. The way the clothes fit his body should be described as obscene, those James Dean jeans and the way his chest and arms fill the fabric of his shirt.

My mouth is watering.

And those eyes....

Cardan Malone is standing in front of me with a smile on his lips.

CHAPTER FOUR

"Fuck my life," I mutter, but the truth is, my heart is pounding hard.

My mouth denies it, at the same time that my skin bristles and something inside me ignites.

"I'm starving," he says as he approaches me, but his eyes speak beyond words. He wants much more than food. "Come have breakfast with me?"

"Just because, by chance, I came to your garage?" I huff. "Appreciate me more than that. I'm here to have my truck's tire fixed. That's it."

He walks up to me like a jaguar, a feline ready to catch its prey. Fine, but I'm not as helpless as he thinks.

"Is there someone here who can take over the job?"

He turns to look behind the counter, where a boy a little younger than me stares at him with his mouth open. "Yes, Mr. Malone, right away."

The boy runs off, and well, just like that, someone is fixing my tire.

"Anything else you need before we go to breakfast?" He looks at me again with those green eyes. "An oil change, tire rotation…"

"I… guess…" I stammer because I can't think of a good excuse.

His smile doesn't fade for an instant. It grows larger when he realizes the state of confusion in which I find myself.

"Leo, I'm going to have breakfast. Call me if you need me," he shouts to another man in the office attached to the reception area.

"The only place I'm going to is to sit on the couch while my tire is getting fixed."

I tell him, passing by his side. Or at least trying to, as Cardan takes my hand and puts a kiss on my cheek very casually.

"Come have breakfast with me," he whispers in my ear. "I can take you wherever you need to go after that."

"What? You have a second job as an Uber driver?"

There it is. I am myself again.

"For you, I'd be whatever you need me to be. Let's go." He takes my hand again, pulling it gently, but I'm not moving from here. It's convenient to invite me to breakfast because the opportunity has fallen into his lap, but no, I won't give in so easily.

It might also be the reason why I'm single, as Dee would say, but that's beside the point.

"La Gloria Orchard," he says, looking into my eyes, when he has realized that my feet are still well planted on the reception floor. "State highway…"

"Yeah, yeah, but that doesn't mean anything," I reply, lifting my chin.

He takes a deep breath before speaking, "It means I was giving you some space. This afternoon I was going to pick you up at your house. You can believe me or not, but it's the truth."

With my face tilted up, it is easy to see it in his eyes. His intense gaze hasn't wavered for an instant. It's impossible not to believe him.

When he sees that I look down, he smiles again because he knows the winner of our first battle.

At the same moment that I nod, accepting my defeat, his smile widens. He takes my hand again and guides me through a side door to the parking lot. I'm glad I put more effort into my outfit today. It was a lucky thing I didn't run into Cardan in one of my usual pair of leggings and a t-shirt.

This time the sign of his midlife crisis isn't here. Instead there's a black Jeep with tinted windows. How do I know it's his? Because he has deactivated the alarm and the lights have come on.

A giggle escapes my lips.

"Dude, you have an issue with cars," I tell him.

"I'm a grease monkey. I like cars; what's the problem?"

"Isn't one enough?"

"Variety is the very spice of life," he answers with a quote from one of William Cowper's poems. Leaning closer, so much so that his beard tickles my neck.

"I hope you're referring to the toppings you put on pizza," I reply, as I make an effort to suppress moving my shoulder rather than succumb to the chill that runs through me.

"Among other things…" he mutters.

"I won't be a notch in your bedpost, Cardan Malone."

We looked at each other for a beat, and then another.

"You should know," he says and it sounds like a warning. It seems as if fire sprouts from his green eyes. "It's true, I like variety, but I'll explain it in a metaphor. I like many ice cream flavors, but I always eat from the same cup."

He steps away to open the car door for me, and with one hand on the small of my back, he helps me settle in. Gives my hand a gentle squeeze before closing the door to get in the driver's seat.

While he does it, I do a quick scan of the car. It smells new and is immaculately clean, except for the sunglasses that rest on the tray and the cellphone charger connected to the USB port. This car might have just left the dealership.

Opening the glove compartment seems too invasive, so my thirst for more will have to be quelled by asking questions, although I'll wait until we are at the restaurant or wherever he wants to take me.

As Cardan drives, neither of us utters a single word, yet other things happen. It's the perfect chance to really look at his profile and the way he moves. One hand on the steering wheel, while the other arm rests on the door. My mind immediately travels, wishing his palm is resting on my thigh. This is a man who works with his hands and knows what to do with them. Heat pools inside me while my mind conjures images of him touching me in the shadows of my room.

My mind is fighting against my body's desires. Thank fuck he stops the car. The time to daydream has ended.

"I made plans to come here this morning," I tell him with a smile pulling up my lips, realizing that he has parked in front of 'Sunny's Café. I'm already craving the pancakes with blueberries and whipped cream, my favorites.

"We're on the same wavelength," he responds, releasing his seat belt while I do the same, ready to get out.

"Whatever you say," I tell him before he walks away and runs to open my door.

Again he is close, too close. And before I can do anything else, his lips are on mine. Cardan Malone is kissing me. Here on the street, where anyone can see us. One hand is at the base of my neck while the other goes down my back until it stays dangerously close to my ass.

And that kiss. It doesn't feel like any I've had before.

His tongue touches mine, and a groan comes out of his throat, and damn my ears because I think it's the best thing they've ever heard.

I would walk on my knees to hell and back for this kiss. My body feels alive—each part of it.

"We're connected," he says, taking his mouth away from mine. Licking his lips, savoring me in his mouth, this isn't fair. I want to yell at him to go back to what we were doing. Why interrupt something that feels so good? Fuck what others think.

You only live once.

His green gaze sweeps my body, staying briefly on my hips as if he were conjuring images of me in his head. Then Cardan surprises me saying, "Let's eat." He takes me by the hand and leads me inside the restaurant.

As always, the place is packed, even for a Monday. We sit under the pergola on the patio at a table for two. The day is cold but sunny. Around the place, they have strategically placed some gas heaters, making it quite pleasant.

He is trying too hard to be Mr. Nice Guy, but now I know he has a dirty mind.

"I've been eating here every day," he tells me, explaining himself.

"Why don't you cook at home? Don't you miss home cooking?" I ask him.

"Are you going to cook for me? That sounds like an invitation." His eyes fixed on mine. I want to lose myself in them. I want to run my hands through his dark beard and know if it feels as good as it looks. I want my fingers gliding along the wave just there.

"You still haven't earned a taste of my Mexican food."

Something I can't describe is drawn on his face. The man knows how to read between the lines. You know what I mean.

"So far," he replies, and I don't say anything. I hope he understands my silence.

I'm opening the door for us to get to know each other better—just a crack, but it's something.

But one thing must be made clear. I'm not making any promises because I'm not in the best place to make them.

I lift my head, looking around. I need to distract myself with something other than him. He would consume me like a moth in the flame. He is too intense.

Too much—him. Period.

Looking around again, a strange sadness invades me. The last time I was here I came with my mother. After Thanksgiving, we had been out shopping for Christmas, and we decided to charge our batteries before starting our marathon.

Remembering that is like a bucket of cold water to my mood.

I reach out to take a drink from my glass of water, trying to get past the lump of tears forming in my throat. I refuse to cry. This has been a good week.

One without tears. I'm not going to spoil it, least of all while being here with him.

Cardan realizes something is happening. It is impossible to hide from that green gaze that seems to see inside me.

"Why did you decide to leave Los Angeles?" I ask after a few minutes of silence.

I have to focus this conversation on him and do what Dee told me.

"Because I was tired of the city. I needed a change."

"The crisis of middle age, they say," I declare with a mocking smile pulling the corners of my lips up.

"I don't know if it is because of my age like you say," he explains. "But I realized I was surrounded by a lot of people, and at the end of the day, I had more cars than friends. So I decided to try my luck elsewhere."

That's sad, but I also realize that my situation isn't much different.

I know a lot of people; everyone here in Sunny Hills is wonderful. But close friends....

Just Destinee.

"And your family?" Information, information. Give me everything I need.

"It's just my mother and me," he tells me. "Well, she remarried. Dick is a good man, so she now has time to focus on bugging me."

Hearing him talk about his mother, my thoughts return to mine.

Wishing that they could sell a ticket back to yesterday or a stairway to heaven because I'm dying to hug her again.

I wish I had known that night would be the last time...

"And ask you for grandchildren," I remember what he told me the day we met.

Cardan stretches his hand across the table, touching mine gently. We are definitely connected because an electric current passes between us, making us vibrate with it.

We stare at each other for a few silent heartbeats, neither wanting to spoil the moment with words.

And, of course, that's when they come to bring our meals.

"It comes with dessert," he tells me when he sees my sweet pancakes topped with cream.

On the other hand, he has ordered the traditional butter ones with eggs, bacon, and ham. Food for half a regiment, at least. Cardan must spend a good amount of time in the gym working out with weights to maintain a figure like his, often.

The idea of an exhaustive workout comes to my mind again. *Calm down. Elena.*

"It's been my favorite," I tell him, focusing on the food that is delicious, by the way. "Since I was a little girl."

He smiles but says nothing with a mouth full of food, it's impossible for him to reply.

While we eat, we go through a variety of topics, the orchard, the garage. His car collection remains a sore spot.

"Did you tell me where you live?" I asked him after a while.

"I'll exchange that information for your phone number," he replies, reaching into his jeans pocket to take out his phone. He opens the app and places it on the table, ready for me to put my contact info in. "Here."

"What? Didn't your Google search tell you everything about me?"

"I only found the information about your orchard, a Facebook profile where you never post anything, no photos of you, unless your friend Destinee decides to tag you in one. You only have things about your mangoes and the fruits that you have started to dehydrate on Instagram. You aren't an easy woman to stalk. Now your phone."

"You didn't answer my question, and a deal is a deal."

He lets out a growl that comes from his chest before answering. "I live above the garage; we turned the second floor of the old station into a loft for me. I'll be delighted to give you a tour."

Too early for that. Sadly true.

"We'll see…"

"I'm going to convince you, Elena. I'm eventually going to convince you."

He has stated it with such confidence that I don't doubt it for a moment. However, my fear is what he wants to do with me.

Will I have the strength to say no?

As I finish typing my number on Cardan's phone, the gadget rings.

"Malone," he answers and pauses to listen to whoever is on the other end of the line with his eyes closed and breathing deeply. "What? What's a cop doing at my business? No… no… offer him a coffee, whatever. Give me ten minutes."

I frown at how little I can make out of the conversation.

Should I be worried?

"I need to head back to the garage," he says, tossing the silverware onto his plate. I guess knowing that the police are looking for you could make anyone lose their appetite.

Mine is gone too.

"I get it," I mutter.

"You have nothing to worry about," he murmurs as he takes my hand back across the table, like my touch calms him down, like something inside him was pushing him to seek that connection again. "Elena, I'm not a felon. My goal here in Sunny Hill is to open a garage to restore vintage cars. This has to be some kind of inspection or a routine visit to check my licenses, some shit like that."

Well, let's hope so because as much as I want to have an adventure, the last thing I want is to end up involved in illegal affairs.

Dirty business? That is another thing.

Ten minutes later, still holding hands, we entered the garage office through the same side door.

And there's Griffin Malone, a local police detective, waiting by the front desk, chatting happily with the same guy who ran out to take care of my truck earlier.

God, what's going on here?

CHAPTER FIVE

Cardan stops, just a heartbeat, takes a deep breath, and runs his hand over his work shirt buttons before continuing to walk like an actor just before entering the scene.

Here we go, and whatever happens, happens.

"How can I help you, officer?" Cardan greets him, extending his hand, and paints a serious expression on his face. When he's alone with me, his face looks different, letting me know what he is thinking.

Or feeling.

Now, it's different. He doesn't show any signs of being nervous, not even when Griffin Malone evaluates him with those dark eyes.

"I'm Detective Malone from the Sunny Hills Police Department." Griffin introduces himself, then he looks at me and smiles. "Elena, how nice to see you again. How's your father?"

Griffin is a nice guy, a lot older than me, I think he graduated high school with my brother Gabriel, but I'm not sure.

"We're all fine, Griffin, thank you," I replied, smiling a little. Cardan looks at me, growls, and turns his attention to Malone.

His hand still holds mine firmly.

"How can I help you, Detective?"

"This isn't an official visit. I didn't come with a search warrant in my possession or anything," Griffin informs him. With that said, I let out a breath of relief, which I didn't even realize I was holding. "The people at my wife's school told me that you were there on Saturday, and I was curious; Malone isn't a very common last name around here."

This time it's Cardan who's questioning it. Has Griffin come to start a pissing contest? That's ridiculous.

"I'm not from the area," Cardan replies dryly.

I'm sure he doesn't like explaining, much less when he doesn't have to.

"I'm sorry I introduced myself like this," he says. "Yesterday—accidentally—you were the topic of conversation while we had dinner at my parents' house and…"

Cardan frowns and gives Griffin a killer look.

"How does someone you don't know—*accidentally*—become the topic of conversation at Sunday's family dinner?" From the way he tightens his hand, I can tell that Cardan is getting more and more upset.

Griffin laughs a little and shakes his head. "Listen, man, it turns out that my father is a man who is proud of his family."

"And what does that have to do with me?" Cardan asks.

"He was commenting something about us being the only Malones in town, which was a complete curse when we were teenagers, you know, three wild boys doing their thing. Emerson, my wife, said that there is a new Malone boy on the block."

Cardan nods, understanding, but he's still not pleased.

"I understand your curiosity, I'm new in town and all that, but I'm not a circus freak to have come and entertain you. Now if you'll excuse me, I'm busy."

Duel of the titans, two alphas ready to face off. Cardan has briefly told Griffin to go back where he came from without explaining, and Griffin refuses to move.

"We started on the wrong foot," Griffin insists and draws a smile to his face as he extends his hand in Cardan's direction. "I'm Griffin Malone; welcome to Sunny Hills."

"Thank you," Cardan reaches out and puts a complacent expression on his face, making it like a greet-my-client type of look.

"Your family, they…" Griffin has changed his strategy; now he's playing good cop.

He keeps persisting on getting answers.

"They are fine, doing their thing…" Nope, Cardan didn't take the bait.

"Are you planning to stay in town for awhile?" Here we go again.

"Does starting a business and investing a lot of money give you a clue, *detective?*"

Griffin lets out a sigh, acknowledging his defeat. Maybe later on things can be better between them, but I doubt it.

"Good luck with your business, Malone," Griffin says goodbye, and I think he used his last name by way of a statement. "It was good to see you again, Lena. Please give my regards to your father."

We both stand in the same spot until Griffin steps out of our line of sight, then Cardan tugs on my hand, "Let's go home."

I don't know how to respond. The invitation has no sexual context as it is more of a statement.

"You aren't going to show me around the garage or something?"

"Do you want to see my lift post?" he asks, barely turning to see me. "You just have to ask if that's what you want."

Why did that sound like pun intended?

We go up some stairs I hadn't seen behind the garage to a wooden door that Cardan opens by typing a code on a small screen.

"Welcome," he says. With a hand on the small of my back, he invites me to come in, holding the door open for me.

The door closes behind me, and my mouth opens. This isn't what I imagined in my head.

Not at all.

It is a beautiful loft, not very big, but it is nice, masculine, and functional. Upon entering, there is a living room with a sectional sofa, and a coffee table made from a tree trunk and glass; beyond the kitchen, there's a bar with two red chairs and a staircase that leads to the second floor. Everything is organized, there is no clutter anywhere, and it is fully furnished. No boy lives here, this is a man's house. Because that's what Cardan is.

"Can I offer you something to drink?" Cardan asks his hand still on my back, gently pushing me.

I nod my head before two words slip from my lips, "Water, please."

I follow him into the kitchen, admiring the rather unusual color palette: cherry red, green, and rustic wood mixed with the concrete wall, the black iron of the large windows to the left, the beams that support the bedroom, and the exposed brick.

I love it.

"I hope you don't like walking naked at night," I say jokingly and immediately regret saying those words.

He turns around, closing the refrigerator. Two bottles of cold water in his hands.

"Thinking of me naked?" he asks, raising an eyebrow. "I like where this is going."

I let out a laugh before I gently rebuke him. "Don't get your hopes up. I was thinking about whether I'll have to save some money to bail you out for public indecency. Anyone who walks near the trees behind the patio can see inside."

He shakes his head. "Elena, the windowpanes have a treatment. No one can see inside, not even at night."

He hands me one of the water bottles, having removed the lid.

"My money is safe then," I tell him, smiling.

Cardan pulls one of the bar chairs away for me to sit down. It's a chivalrous gesture, and I don't know why I'm surprised.

"Why didn't you want to answer Griffin's questions?"

"Straight to the point," he answers with a smile on his lips, but there is no joy in his gesture; it is rather bitter. "I didn't answer because I didn't have to. My private life is that, private."

I think about Griffin. I've known him my whole life. Here in Sunny Hills, everyone knows who he is.

"Griffin is a good guy, and his family is quite involved in the community. Logically, I can see why he was curious."

He stares at me intensely in silence for a couple of seconds.

"Why are you defending him? Elena, he was not the only one who has come here to give me a lecture on how my new and brilliant business is absorbing the previous clientele. Do you think I didn't have some opposition when I asked for the licenses? But I'm a businessman and honest. I'm not one of those who believe in doing cheap work for stealing someone else's business. I may have been lucky, but deep down, I'm just a grease monkey like any other."

Shit, I didn't know that. Now I can understand why he raises his defenses.

And I highly doubt that luck had anything to do with all this that he has built. This speaks of hard work and a lot of organization.

"I am not defending Griffin, and although I think he should have warned the person who called you to let you know that it was not an official visit, I don't think his intentions were bad. As I said, Griffin is a good guy, and so is his family. Or do you have something to hide?"

He looks back at me silently, his eyes slightly narrowed. He takes a long swallow of the water as if he needed liquid courage. Well, might it be water, it might be tequila, whatever helps.

"I was born in Chicago; my mother is from there. We lived there for a while, after that, we moved to Los Angeles, I'm sure she did it to please my idiot father. He disappeared within two months, leaving her with a mess of unpaid debts and a baby to feed. All I have of him is his name on my birth certificate. Sorry I don't want to share that information with the entire town. It's my life, Elena."

This time, I'm the one who takes a long drink from the water bottle.

"Sorry," I tell him sincerely. My heart sinks, his father's last name was Malone. It seems completely acceptable that he doesn't want to talk about him. And even if that wasn't the case, he said it. It is his life. "But let me give you some advice. Small towns are a wonderful place to live; people are friendly and care about each other. The bad news is that everyone gets involved in one way or another."

He finishes his water before saying. "Duly noted."

I want to change the subject and cheer him up.

"I had no idea this space was hiding in this old station." That's the truth. The place that they have transformed into their modern garage had been abandoned since I was a child.

"You can thank the company I hired to remodel the place," he gets up and walks over to the green velvet sectional chair that rests on the hardwood floor of the living room. "Of all this, there are only two things that I brought. I bought that lamp from an artist in Los Angeles, the man has more talent than money, and I wanted to help him." He points to the teak beams where a curious steel structure hangs. "And my bed, you can guess the reasons."

He walks to the window to gaze out at the grove that extends beyond the confines of his backyard. Before I can stop myself, my feet are doing the same, until I'm standing right next to him.

"I like your house, Cardan Malone."

Cardan turns around, looking at me with those electrifying green eyes. "I like you."

His words take my breath away. My body thrums.

"Don't insist on denying it, Elena," he says, approaching me. His work boots almost touch mine as he leans over me. Our mouths only a few inches apart. He's so tall, I can't see any further, his broad shoulders blocking everything. "I can feel your desire, believe me when I tell you that you aren't alone."

I stare at him for a moment, my feet kicking back a bit. What he said is true, however....

"I'm not going to lie, I'm not used to doing it," I start to speak. "I'm attracted to you, but I don't know if I like you, at least not yet."

A slow smile plays on his lips.

Damn conceited man.

"Let's find out together, Elena," he murmurs. I can feel his breath on my lips, my mouth inches from kissing him. "Let me show you what I'm capable of."

Bossy man. And I'm already getting used to it.

Cardan Malone is fire. Should I succumb to the flames? Maybe I want to burn…

But what he doesn't know is that there are reasons why I should fight.

There is no future for us, I can't commit beyond today.

"Say yes," he insists. Those eyes don't stop looking into mine.

I swear he can see to the bottom of my soul, where I have never let anyone else in.

"Is my truck ready?" I ask, the words rushing out of my mouth. "I have to go home."

"Let's go get your truck, I'm sure it's waiting for you."

He takes my hand and doesn't let it go until he closes the door after helping me up, making sure I've put my seat belt on and everything else.

"See you soon," is the last thing I hear him say, and those words have sounded like a challenge to me.

♡♡♡

I'm opening my kitchen door when my phone rings.

I know exactly what I need, a distraction. My father should be in the orchard, supervising the few workers we have at this time of year.

The phone keeps ringing, but I don't want to answer. I really want to take advantage of the fact there's nobody home and draw up a defense strategy. Focus. Yes, that's what I need.

It isn't harvest season yet as we pick the mangoes in the summer. During that time, we will be tremendously busy, so it would be good for me to get some work done. I want to sell mangoes with chili as a snack on the go—small, sealed bags with the delicacy inside.

I walk to the pantry and grab about four pounds of dried chili peppers that I bought a few days ago at the farmer's market. I have already washed and dried them in the sun. It's a ton, but it's nice to have my very own chili powder mix to season my dehydrated mangoes.

I know there are many options on the market and that I could buy it ready-to-go. But I realized something while I have been experimenting with this, and it's that the taste of the powder makes a big difference. I'm determined to have the best from day one.

From one of the drawers, I take out the largest frying pan I have at home. After letting it heat for a few seconds, I toss the first chiles on the surface. This time, I will mix four different types, it is my favorite combination, and I'm sure it will be a success.

I like this. It's my thing. And it's the only thing that has kept me from thinking about the future.

My business. Something other than the farm that I will one day inherit from my father. After losing my mother, I don't even want to think about it. My father is a healthy and strong man, and he will be with me for many more years.

When the first chiles are brown on both sides, I remove them from the heat and put them on a tray that I have ready to one side. This is just the beginning, I am sure I will be out here roasting all afternoon.

Works for me.

My phone rings again. I have assigned a very special ringtone to whoever is calling. To know when to avoid them, like right now.

Destinee.

About two hours have passed, time has given me much more than I expected, and in these minutes, I have only thought about Cardan Malone and what he told me only about two million times.

Fucking man.

Why isn't he one of those men who want a quickie in the bathroom and continues on his way like nothing happened?

Why does he want something I can't offer?

The time to grind the peppers has come. I have a fairly large food processor, which will make the task easier for me, at the moment that I'm rinsing it under the stream of warm water from the kitchen sink, I hear the door close and a voice that I know very well shouting to me.

"Bitch," she calls out, but I refuse to even turn around.

There is no use, it's better to just let her be. Maybe I'll get lucky, and she'll eventually tire out and leave me alone.

"Now tell me already if Cardan Malone was the one you went out for breakfast this morning at Sunny's Cafe," she says firmly. Oh great, my luck seemed to have run out on me today. "And why didn't you call me up right away to tell me about it?"

"Wow," I murmur in disbelief as her interrogations linger on. "Gossip travels fast around here, doesn't it?"

Her pale azure eyes roll in annoyance before settling on me again. "It's been all over the Facebook group for hours! Though I know I shouldn't believe those rumors, when they asked me about it, I had to say that I would be the first one to know if it were true since I'm your bestie! So now I'm giving you the chance to set things straight."

"Wait a second," Dee interjects with a dramatic flair of her arm. "No one thought to click some photos, too? Phones come with high-resolution cameras nowadays any person; can easily immortalize the moment without getting caught!"

I arch an eyebrow skeptically at her statement. That is certainly my friend Dee.

"What do you mean no documented proof?" she continues.

A giggle escapes my lips, seemingly uncontrollable. "Wow, now I feel pretty safe about my privacy and all that."

Destinee moves through my kitchen like it was her home, and she's welcome here. She pours herself a cup of cold coffee and flops onto a chair around the table at the foot of the window.

"Privacy doesn't exist in the era of social media, now speak. Pleading the fifth is not going to work here."

She takes her phone out of her pants back pocket while she waits for an answer.

"What the hell are you doing? You came to make me spill the beans or burn your eyelashes on that appliance. Give me good news because as you can see, I'm busy."

I put some of the roasted chiles in the food processor, close the lid carefully and begin to grind until they become a powder. In this step, you can grind them as much as you want, but for the mangoes, I need them powdered. And the noise keeps Destinee's lips sealed.

"Hell, that smells good," she says, approaching the container as soon as I take it out of the processor.

Of course, she can't even wait two seconds. It's like a girl in front of freshly baked cookies.

"Shit," she squeals as she coughs over and over. There it is. You have to wait for the powder to settle before opening the lid.

"Dee, this isn't the first time…" I scold her as she takes another sip of her coffee, trying to mitigate the effects of the chili powder.

I look at her blonde hair in a ponytail, her blue eyes are full of tears.

Damn girl should know better by now.

"Are you going to tell me or what?"

"Are you going to drop the phone or what?"

"Wait, I found him," she announces, flipping to show me what she has there. Cardan's Instagram profile. "Tell me this isn't Cardan Malone and that you aren't interested at all."

"Don't tell me you were stalking him?"

She makes a theatrical gesture, opening her mouth, putting her hand to her chest, and everything.

As if she didn't know her….

"Of course not, women don't spy. We investigate."

I roll my eyes, "Obviously."

"Now, stop making a racket with that thing and tell me everything."

Maybe it's good to get all this off my chest. After all, she's my friend, and any advice couldn't hurt.

CHAPTER SIX

"I just don't understand why you won't give the guy a chance," is the first thing that comes out of Destinee's mouth after telling her my story, miraculously without interruption.

"Because what can I offer him?" I tell her before getting up from the table as I need to start cooking something for dinner. I'm sure my dad will come in hungry.

"Lena, don't start with those stupid arguments again," she chides me. As I said before, she knows everything about my life, and this isn't the first time we have had this conversation. "Your life is not over, and it's you who is limiting it."

Boom.

Boom.

Boom.

Those words hit me right in the chest.

These last few weeks haven't been easy. I haven't been making any decisions lightly.

And it's tiring that those around me feel they have the right to judge me.

Nobody can because nobody has walked in my shoes.

"You're scared," she tells me, again accusing me.

Of course, I'm scared, anyone in my position would be shitting bricks.

"No shit, Sherlock."

I take some chicken breasts from the refrigerator. They are marinated and ready to put in the oven, I sprinkle some of the chili powder that I just ground because I know my father loves spicy food. We'll also have mashed potatoes and fresh salad for dinner. At the farmer's market, I got the most wonderful combination of vegetables last weekend, and I am determined to feed my father as healthy as I can.

And this offers me something else to focus on, something other than the lecture my friend is giving me.

"What about your father?"

My hands stop. She has no right to go there.

"He's already heartbroken, Lena. How do you think he feels knowing you've already given up?"

I turn around to face her, flames coming out from my eyes, but Destinee doesn't even blink when she sees my rage. What's more, from her expression, I can swear she sought to provoke me.

"Dax said nothing might happen for years…" I remind her, and she knows that well. She was there with me holding my hand.

"My brain is an endless source of wisdom. See? Years and years of adventures to live."

Here I am ready to score a point: game, set, match. "And that's what I'm doing, in case you don't remember I just jumped from a plane just a few days ago and I have plans to keep doing things for me."

Ha! She stays quiet as she has no arguments to refute that.

"I hope you realize that there is more to you than that." She ends the discussion, knowing I will not change my mind. "Now tell me you're going to make me a snack with that powder with which you almost killed me. I just finished my shift at the hospital, and I'm beat."

To emphasize what was said, my friend kicks off her sneakers, rolls the chair in front of her, and lifts her feet.

I'm still upset, and this feeling of uneasiness will take time to fade, that's a sure fact.

"When did you get so cynical?" she asks me while looking at me like I grew another head. "You were the romantic one of us two, Lena. Do you remember when we were just little girls, and you asked your mother to take you to San Francisco so you could throw the bottle with your letter to the love of your life? You were the only eight-year-old girl who waited for Valentine's Day instead of writing to Santa Claus. How many years have you been doing it?"

So many, I think, but I don't tell her anything. I don't want to encourage her.

That memory makes me smile. I was pestering my mother for days until she agreed to take me. he following year, we did the same, making it our little tradition.

From the refrigerator, I grab a cucumber, peel it, and cut it into thick strips; after arranging it on a plate with a few lemon slices, I sprinkle chili and put it in front of Destinee, who looks at it like manna, which fell from the sky.

"I'm not giving you anything else before dinner," I point my finger at her to emphasize what I've said. "And don't even try to protest."

When the sun begins to fall on the horizon, my father opens the door and enters the kitchen, he smiles when our gazes meet. I've already taken care of the potatoes, and now the glass tray with the mash is in the oven with some cheese.

"Wow, you're a sight for sore eyes," he says before kissing me on the cheek and then walking over to Dee to do the same. It's not weird, or anything like that, my father sees my best friend as another daughter. "And something smells delicious."

We had dinner, laughing just like old times. Well, kinda, because before my mother would also be here with us, or one of my brothers.

But there is no going back, the past is past.

"Martina told me they have good strawberries on their farm," my father tells me as he finishes eating, referring to someone we have known for years. Well, in Sunny Hills, everyone has known each other forever. "I asked her for several boxes for you. I thought maybe you would like to use the device that you bought, I mean, before the mango season begins."

That makes me smile, that's my father. Always so considerate.

"Do you want to pick them out tomorrow?"

"Of course, I do," I answer, taking his hand and giving it a gentle squeeze. In response, he gives me a wink.

Around nine o'clock, Dee gets up to leave. "I would gladly stay, but tomorrow I start my shift early at the hospital. I have Saturday off; we could do something fun. How about we go to Napa for a spa day?"

Napa, a spa, quiet time. Manicure and pedicure.

Some dinner. A lot of wine.

That sounds wonderful.

"I'll take care of the reservations," she says as she opens the kitchen door to leave. A few feet away, her bright red Corolla awaits her.

"Crazy girl, I haven't said yes."

She turns a little to look at me over her shoulder, still walking. "I know you well, the answer was written all over your face. I'm going to add full waxing to the list, something tells me you're going to need it very soon."

Sex. I thought I had lost interest until a cocky man with green eyes and a thick beard decided to come my way.

♡♡♡

My father and I spent the next morning checking the planting of the trees on the lot we recently bought. This is my life, walking among green leaves and waiting for the branches to bear fruit. I love being here, this is my happy place.

And with my new project, I hope to give even more life to this company, which, thanks to the payment plan to buyout my brothers, one day it will all be mine.

We left an area near the creek untouched. My father knows that it is my favorite place, and a few months ago, he suggested that the day I decide to start a family, I could build my own home in that area. At the time, it seemed like a wonderful idea. Now, I don't know if that is possible.

Future. What to do when fate takes it out of your hands?

Without giving it much thought, I let these words come out of my mouth, "I'm going to see Dax, *papá*."

For a few minutes, he doesn't say anything, and I think his brain short-circuits, but knowing my father as well as I do, he's giving me time, respecting my space and the way I function.

And also giving me the opportunity to be the one to explain this decision that although it's sudden, he has been waiting for weeks.

"As soon as I get home, I'm going to call his office to make an appointment," I tell him.

"You know you don't need to do that; you could just show up at the hospital."

That makes me laugh, "Are you afraid I will regret it?"

Neither of us pauses, we keep moving among the young trees that provide no shade, and even though it's not hot this time of year, in the California Valley we rarely have a cloudy day. The weather is inclement.

"I have tried to stay out of it, respecting whatever you decide to do. Even when it's difficult for me to do it."

"I know," I agree, we both crouch near a tree whose roots appear dangerously bare. We're going to have to come over this afternoon and fix this.

"What made you change your mind?" he asks me in a low voice.

I take a deep breath, stand up, and brush my hands on the fabric of my jeans. "I haven't, at least not yet." I'm being completely honest with him, and I know he doesn't like my answer. "But I also think I can give it a try. I want to know my options."

My father smiles. This time little wrinkles form around his dark eyes so similar to mine. Even in his sixties he is a very handsome man, he and my mother made a beautiful couple. They were admired—and envied—by many people in town.

"I know you are an adult now, Lena, but to me, you will always be the little girl who was delivered to me wrapped in a pink blanket at the hospital," as he said it, his eyes water. "Do you want me to go with you?"

Damn, the last thing I want is for my father to get emotional, so my next words try to ease the situation.

"What? So you can harass me with what you hear Dax says?"

My father lets out a laugh that echoes in the field.

"You know me well."

"Since the day I was born. I'll let you know when I make the appointment."

When we return home, we each go our separate ways. My father goes in search of the SUV to go harass the workers about the work they are doing, and I lock myself in the office. It's Tuesday, and I have to prepare the payroll for the end of the period. Although our staff is small at this time of year, I don't like having work pile up. I also need to prepare the documentation to send to our accountant, tax season is approaching, and nobody wants to have the IRS breathing down their necks. It's every businessman's nightmare.

Death and taxes. Two unavoidable subjects.

My stomach growls as I look at the clock. It's past noon. I should have listened to my father and had more than a cup of coffee for breakfast this morning. But I wasted enough time drying my hair and work starts early in the orchard. Our land isn't very big, but it seems that it multiplies when we have so much preparation to do.

I get up and walk down the short hallway that leads from my office to the kitchen, the wooden floor creaks under my boots. I have lived in this house all my life and find it comforting. For many, it may seem childish that I didn't leave the nest, but now I am glad, I would have missed it a lot if I'd left.

I'm about to open the refrigerator when I hear someone knock on the front door. The knocks are strong, but not desperate.

It's weird, we don't usually have visitors, and Destinee invites herself in, usually coming through the kitchen door, yelling at me.

My jaw almost falls to the floor when I open the door to meet the man who's been invading my thoughts recently. He's there, smiling at me, holding a paper bag in one of his hands, while with the other, he leans over the wooden door frame, towering over me.

Those jeans must be custom-made, otherwise I can't understand how they all fit so well. The cocky version of James Dean, in a work shirt and boots.

Why the hell didn't I put a little more effort getting ready this morning?

I'm wearing my old, ripped jeans, work boots, and a gray long-sleeved shirt that has seen better days. My hair is in a high ponytail and not a stitch of makeup on.

"What are you doing here?" Wow, the first thing that comes out of my mouth is a nice welcoming sentence.

He looks at me with eyes full of humor.

"After having breakfast together several times, I thought it was time to upgrade to lunch, so here I am."

Lifting the paper bag a little higher, he emphasizes his point.

"Are you going to invite me in, or do you want us to go to my house?" he mutters, approaching me dangerously. The aroma of his cologne engulfs me, it is intoxicating. I want to pack it in a bottle to put it on my pillow every night. "Maybe make dessert a little more interesting."

This man is like a racing car, as soon as his engine is warmed up, there's no stopping him.

"My father is coming home for lunch. I can't just leave him to eat alone…" I say as an excuse, backing up a bit, with the intention of closing the door, but he takes it as an invitation to enter my house.

"Hope you like a good Reuben. I also brought one for your father."

His smile widens, knowing it took me by surprise. Someone must have spilled the beans at the deli because he brought my father's favorite sandwich.

"Are you going to invite me in for lunch or not, Elena?"

"Do you still need to ask for permission when you already have your body in the house?"

"But you didn't invite me to stay."

"Well, that depends on what else is in the bag."

He leans forward again, enough to whisper in my ear. "I'm a resourceful man, and I did my homework."

I don't doubt it for an instant.

At that very moment, someone, I'm a hundred percent sure who it is, clears his throat behind me. I blush to the very roots of my hair, which doesn't happen very often.

"Mr. Posada," says Cardan, straightening his back, switching the bag to his other hand, and extending his hand to greet my father. "It is a pleasure to finally meet you. Cardan Malone, at your service."

My father evaluates Cardan for a few seconds, in my head I can hear the hands of an imaginary clock tick. Like waiting for a judge to make his sentence.

This *is* an important moment, after all, he's meeting my father.

Cardan isn't stupid. He came to the lion's den prepared, surely since he brought the food for my dad, and must know that I am his only daughter and that for him—as he told me a while ago—I will always be his little girl.

"Mr. Malone," my dad finally says, his tone serious. Without any emotion. "I've heard about you around town."

From the corner of my eye, I see Cardan's jaw clench but forces it to relax a heartbeat later.

"I hope all good things," he replies as I say nothing, but somehow, I know the answer. They all believe that Cardan is a scammer who has come to steal the 'hometowners' business. His situation must not be easy, the newcomer trying to win the trust of people who reject him.

And that speaks volumes of his character, of his determination, of his steel resolve.

"I prefer to make my own judgments." That's my father, a fair man who knows what it means to work hard and respects the value of others' work.

I have always been proud to be his daughter.

"Can I tip the balance in my favor by offering you lunch?" Cardan asks, raising his eyebrows a little.

And here I am, in front of my father, more or less, drooling for this man. And not from the prospect of having my sandwich.

"Let's go to the kitchen." My father invites him in, waving his arm. I walk ahead of them, trying to keep my heart rate under control.

Kick ass, Elena. Be awesome.

Once they are seated around the table, I keep myself busy carrying glasses and plates from the cabinets. Luckily, I have a pitcher of lemonade I made from dried lemon pulp that I got from a neighbor in the refrigerator.

The word is already spreading among the people who know me about my business plans, and they are all willing to pitch in where they can.

The three of us gobbled up the sandwiches Cardan brought—note to self, the man definitely did his homework—at the deli, they know I'm unable to resist their Reuben, their Russian dressing is the best I've ever had. It's not like I've traveled the world to check it out, but when I like something, I like it.

My father doesn't say anything at first, he eats in silence as usual, but as soon as he puts his napkin on the plate, I fasten my imaginary seat belt. Preparing for what is to come.

Third-degree is about to begin.

And knowing how Cardan feels about sharing his private life with strangers, I'm not expecting anything good.

"What brings you to town, boy?" my dad asks him.

Cardan wipes his mouth with his napkin before answering. "I was looking for a location that was attractive enough to open a new branch of my business. Close to a big city, without being in the metropolitan area, and that was also cheap to expand. My interest in coming here has not been to bankrupt anyone; on the contrary, I am interested in putting Sunny Hills on the map for bikers and collectors. Because what I want is that, to focus on the restoration of old cars."

My father looks at him with raised eyebrows as he falls back, leaning back on his seat.

"That is an ambitious plan," he tells Cardan.

"I *am* an ambitious man," Cardan replies, his gaze fixed on my father's eyes.

My father is old-fashioned, and he appreciates someone who can answer him truthfully. We all have secrets, and in no way do I expect Cardan to tell my father his whole life story, of course not. However, I'm grateful and appreciate the effort he is making.

After all, it seems he scored some points by bringing lunch.

I relax as I chew, enjoying the view. Those biceps are a sight to behold. Yes, yes, I know my father is sitting at the table with us, so cut me some slack.

I finish my Reuben happily and start eating the chips one by one. Cardan looks at me from time to time, those green eyes I love so much shining with mischief. He knows what he's done, he knows I'm starting to like him. Quite a bit.

Smartass.

"Mr. Malone, do you like fishing?" my father asks, and I know where things are going.

"Of course, sir," he replies. "And it's Cardan."

My father gets up, picks up his plate, and carries it to the sink. Cardan follows closely, smart man.

"In my office, I have some baits I would like to show you. We bought a piece of land north of the orchard that borders the creek..." My father puts his hand on Cardan's shoulder, inviting him not so subtly to walk down the hall.

Dad kisses me on the cheek, and before walking away, he says, "Thanks for the lemonade. It's delicious as always."

As I watch as they walk down the hall, I wonder how a day that started like all the others took such an amazingly unexpected turn.

The answer pops up like a neon sign.

It's all because of Cardan Malone.

CHAPTER SEVEN

While my father and Cardan are busy talking about bait, I do what every girl in my position would do.

I run to my room to do two things: go and check how I look, and then call my best friend. Destinee will know what to do in a situation like this because the truth of the matter is that I can't think of anything.

Of course, as this is an emergency, the phone goes straight to her voicemail. Dee must be working, and when she's in the hospital, she hardly answers. She better not complain about how she is the last to know.

I succumb to temptation and look carefully at all the photos on Cardan's profile. He has only uploaded a couple, too bad. But the few he has posted are billboard worthy. The others are photos of vintage cars, his own. Other marketing images from a garage in Los Angeles and things like that.

Fuck, I can't spend all day here hiding, just ogling his photos, as much as I want to.

I look at myself in the mirror, measuring the magnitude of the disaster. Changing my clothes is out of the question; it would show too much effort.

Instead, I change my bra for one that makes my boobs look perkier. I put on my favorite moisturizing lotion. The aroma is subtle, not so noticeable. Then I brush my hair and tie it up in a ponytail, a little concealer on the bags under my eyes and some mascara.

And whatever happens, happens.

I go to my office to try to work while they continue their conversation, but as much as I have spent the last five minutes looking at my computer screen, I can't concentrate on anything. What is my father saying to Cardan?

He isn't telling him, would he?

My father wouldn't dare. After all, it's not his secret to tell.

I drop my head on the keyboard, feeling defeated. Life was easier last week.

And that reminds me, I still have to call Dax Pearson's office. But my resolution is weak… I don't want to.

I wish I had the determination to show up at the doctor's office unannounced, but I'm not like that.

It's not who I am.

This time I text Dee.

Elena: *Dinner at my house at 7.*
The eagle has landed.

Not even two minutes have passed when I get one back.

Destinee: *What the fuck does that mean?*

Elena: *See you tonight?*

Destinee: *Elena Maria Posada, don't even think about leaving me hanging like this, I have to work!*

Elena: *See you tonight, don't be late.*

I am sure that as soon as her shift at the hospital is over, I will have my friend here. Knowing her she won't even stop by her house to change.

I drop my head on the back of the burgundy velvet chair, leaning back, looking at the gray walls of the small room like all the answers to life's questions are written on them, searching for imaginary cobwebs to have something else to focus on.

My memories fly to the letters that I wrote all those years ago, without caring about the pollution I was contributing to.

There is a knock on the door, and the noise startles me.

"Come in," I say without turning to the door. I know perfectly well who is knocking.

"So, this is where the magic happens?" says that hoarse voice that I like so much. The random question makes me smile.

"What does that mean?"

"I don't know, but I wanted to say it." We both let out a laugh that echoes off the walls of the room. It's nothing to write home about, a white desk and a bookcase the same color that my mother and I found in an antique store, on the floor, a gray and wine-colored rug covering the wood completes the space.

I have many photos in the bookcase – from the whole family in the orchard, to my brothers' graduations, and some of Destinee and myself.

"Can I sit?" he asks me, but there is nowhere to do it. He comes around the desk and leans on it, facing me, looking at me with his hands gripping the wooden surface on either side of his body.

Those arms, I have them less than two feet away, and I want to put my fingers on them and find out if they feel as good as they look.

"Elena," he says to me, and his voice sounds like a warning, the scent of his cologne enveloping us like a cloud that I want to never dissipate.

"Why are you here?" I ask him as he reaches over and strokes his thumb against my cheek.

I want him to stop touching me like that. Right now.

I'd rather he just take me in his arms and kisses me.

"Since we're moving forward with this meal schedule thing," he begins. "How about we go to dinner on Saturday? A client told me about this place near here that…"

I look at him for a moment; in the daylight in my office, he looks even more handsome, bigger. Like he's taking up all the space, and I can't focus on anything else. But nuh-uh. I've already made plans, and I'm not going to cancel them. And I'm sure we'll stay the night in Napa. After a few glasses of wine, neither Dee nor I are going to be fit to drive. And responsibility is above all.

"'Sorry, but plans had been made. I'm not available on Saturday," I say, avoiding eye contact because I'm sure I will change my mind if I do.

"Something I should be concerned about?" he asks me, raising his eyebrows. Damn, those eyes…

"Save some bail money. Knowing Destinee, we will need it."

"A date with your best friend?" I don't know where he got that information from, but it doesn't matter. I can see that while people might not share much about their life, they don't seem to have a problem talking about mine.

"Yes, a girl's day." Perfect time to spill some tea. "We haven't done it in a long time, and we both need it."

He looks at me, and again the rough tip of his finger gently traces my features. I want to put that finger in my mouth and bite it. And then...

"You don't need a trip to the spa," I'm sure he would approve of what I'm plotting to do with him. "If you want a massage, all you have to do is call me."

Yes, yes, a massage, preferably with a happy ending.

"Thanks for the offer," I say as I get up from the chair, this conversation is getting dangerous. "I could check my schedule to see when I'm available."

My cheeky answer makes him smile.

"Have dinner with me," he insists, grabbing me by the waist. Those hands feel so good on me. Even if a thin layer of cotton

"What? You want to see me with makeup, a tight dress, and behaving perfectly all night?"

That makes him laugh.

"It sounds good. But how about you wear whatever you want, and we have a private dinner?"

Damn, the man knows the perfect words to say at the right time.

"A date where you are going to show up at my door with flowers and chocolates?"

"And in the end, you are going to reward me with a kiss on the porch before your father opens the door carrying a gun bursting our bubble."

This is where people insert those famous words, it's not you, it's me.

"I already have plans for this weekend, sorry."

"And you can't include me in them?"

No, unless he has a vagina, and it seems to me that he comes rather armed with a good package, so no.

"I don't think so," I reply.

"You are going out with me." That is not a question; rather it sounds like a challenge.

"We'll see about that, cowboy."

"I'm a man who's used to getting his way, Elena." When he finishes saying this, he stands up, kisses me on the forehead—like it was the most normal thing in the world—and leaves.

I stay in the chair with my mouth open, feeling the blood run furiously through my body, and I swear, I still feel the heat of his lips on my skin.

Worst part?

I want more.

♡♡♡

"I don't understand. How come those sorts of things never happen to me?" Dee asks me as she chews her chicken pasta with chipotle sauce, one of my specialties.

"You are waiting for your oil tycoon," I reply, pointing at her with my fork.

"A tech entrepreneur," she corrects me with a frown, but her words resonate in my head. Maybe she chose the wrong Posada brother. When we were younger, she and my brother Martin were like two peas in a pod. What happened is a mystery to me. "Tech. Entrepreneur. Like those that populate Silicon Valley. Maybe I should move. You never listen to what I tell you."

I know what happened. David happened.

"Lena? Are you listening to me?"

Oh dang, what did she just say? Dee is my best friend, but she talks way too much.

"If you didn't change your mind so much, it might be easier to follow you."

"Whatever," she defends herself before stuffing more spaghetti into her mouth. "If you don't want him, I'll keep him."

Mm, no, I think I like the man, even when I won't admit it out loud.

"You know, we could start a catfight for him," she laughs. "You know, I'm a hair puller."

That makes me laugh. It's just the two of us in the kitchen as my father took dinner to his study. I think it was a polite way of giving my friend and I space to talk.

"Are you also going to scratch me?"

She examines her nails carefully before answering. "First, we have to go to the spa. I need a Nikki Minaj manicure. After that, we'll see, then yes, as long as they don't damage my gel tips."

She's crazy, she's a nurse, long, well-groomed nails don't mix well with her profession.

"I make no promises. That beard deserves a good fight..."

Her saying those words, the image of Cardan Malone appears in my head, him and how tall he is.

Him and those green eyes that I want to devour me.

Him and that beard that I want to feel between my legs.

"Those dreamy little eyes tell me you're not exactly thinking about our trip to the spa on Saturday," Destinee's voice interrupts my heated reverie. "Don't worry, best friend, I have everything under control. I've already made the appointment, and complete waxing is definitely on your list."

Cardan and I have been hanging around each other, but he has been very reserved and measured with his physical intimacy, content with the pace. Now the question is how soon would he put that waxing to good use.

"Here's hoping all your hard work pays off," I say with a sly wink.

"But let's get real. I haven't even had the pleasure of meeting this man yet. All I know is that you're going to be sittin' on a mighty fine reward if all goes well." Destinee muses while inspecting her fingernails. "You'd be hard-pressed to find someone like Cardan Malone. But something tells me you just might get a big fat reward like a billion times over."

My money's on it. A guy like Cardan Malone doesn't make promises he can't keep.

"You know what? This is where you're supposed to say that he's too old for me and that this spring chicken needs fresh meat!"

She bursts out laughing at my lame joke. Typical.

"Girl, don't be silly now—you're not sixteen or something like that! We aren't talking about pedophilia here—twelve years is the perfect age gap; the man has twelve years of experience for ya!"

She scours his Instagram profile with a hungry eye, and we both ooh and ah over the detailed shoulder tattoos and the intricate lines inked onto his arm.

"Tell me his best friend is a tech mogul from Silicon Valley."

"I don't know," I reply, and that's the truth. "Cardan speaks very little of his friends." Or his life in general.

"Because he's trying to get something from you. I'd suggest you get him drunk and make him fall at your feet."

"It terrifies me to think that I'm going out with you for the weekend. Your sanity is clearly questionable, and my security…"

She looks at me open-mouthed, as if I just offended her principles. My eyes are rolling almost by reflex. This girl…

"You're going to have fun. I guarantee it."

That is what I want, to close my eyes and have fun, forget that my problems will be here waiting for me.

Destinee and I continue eating, basically in silence, until I am the one who breaks it.

"I told my father that I would call Dax this week, but I haven't found the courage to do so." While words left my lips, my friend's face turns serious immediately. Destinee knows how hard it is for me to do this. Plus, as an RN, the person who is always taking care of others, her seriousness coming out.

"I could go to his office tomorrow before my shift. I'm sure I can accommodate you without any issue," she suggests.

"My father told me that Dax practically has a place ready for me as soon as I decide to call him: hat I'm not sure is if the fear that consumes me is ready to recede."

Destinee extends her hand across the table to take mine, squeezing it gently but firmly. "You know you aren't alone, Lena. I'll be there in case you don't want to go alone.

Also, you know that at the time of the exams and any other treatments you decide to take, I'll be your personal nurse or your nanny. Whatever you need."

My heart clenches in my chest. So I have to lighten the mood before I burst into tears. I miss my mother, I haven't recovered from the battle of losing her, and now I must face a new challenge.

"Eww… no personal nurse," I chide her, reaching out for the glass of wine that's in front of my plate.

"You little pervert, that's not what I meant. Anyway, you know you're not alone, right? And surely your father has told you the same. So are you going to call Dax tomorrow?"

"Probably," I answer as confidently as I can. "I don't know yet."

After all, tomorrow is still a workday, and she has an early morning shift, and I have to go with my father to supervise the compost delivery we ordered last week to fertilize the trees while our workers finish the planting.

Two hours later, 'freshly off the shower, I'm sitting crisscross on the bed, drying my long dark hair, when my phone chimes.

Tell me that you are awake and thinking of me.

It can't be other than Cardan Malone, that fucking cocky man.

Elena: *Someone is very full of himself.*

In less than two seconds, my heart races when I see the little dots dancing on my phone screen.

Cardan: *So, were you thinking of me?*
Elena: *Any particular reason I should be?*

I can almost hear him laughing from here, that husky laugh I enjoy so much.

Cardan: *Because I'm the most handsome man you've ever seen, isn't that reason enough?*

Elena: *The most arrogant, without a doubt.*

Cardan: *That didn't answer my question. Tell me you were thinking of me.*
Because let me say that you have serious competition.

Elena: *Competition?*

Cardan: *Serious competition.*

A few days ago, I met a mysterious girl who is looking for adventure, and I can't get her out of my head.

That makes me smile. I settle in better, stretching my legs and tucking them under the soft covers that cover my bed as I rest my back on the pillows and the wooden headboard.

Elena: *Tell me more. If there's competition, I want to know my enemy better.*

Cardan: *A beautiful brunette who makes me chase her all over town.*

Oh, I like where this is going.

Elena: *Are you sure you're talking about a girl and not a German shepherd?*

Cardan: *Sure, maybe I should get a dog. It would give me some love.*

Elena: *Maybe you need to improve your game, Malone. You seem to be losing your touch.*

Cardan: *You've set the challenge, Bonita.*

Elena: *Now, are you talking to me in Spanish?*

Cardan: *What? Are you asking me to talk dirty to you? Let me tell you, dirty is my second language.*

Elena: *This better not be the part where you send me a dick pic; forget it.*

Cardan: *Are you asking me for a dick pic, Elena?*

Elena: *I think you are delirious.*

Cardan: *Nothing to be ashamed of. There is much to love here.*

Thank God I'm alone in my room, with no one around. Otherwise, I couldn't be carrying this conversation without blushing.

Cardan: *And after showing you the family jewels. It's time for you to show me the goods.*

Ha! Keep dreaming.

Elena: *I don't think you have heard of that thing called privacy. My photos will not be circulating on the net tomorrow.*

Cardan: I promise you that your privacy is safe with me.

Elena: Doesn't your neck hurt sometimes?

Cardan: What the hell are you talking about?

Elena: To carry that big head, smartass.

Cardan: My neck is fine, thank you, all my psyche is proportioned.
Do you want to see it for yourself?

Elena: The user of this line is not available.

Cardan: Very funny.
Cardan: I like you.

Oh, Cardan, and I like you. But this is not the time yet.

Elena: Why? You don't know me.

Cardan: I've learned to trust my guts. I like you, and that's it.

Even miles away, he makes me feel things inside, but the time has come to end this conversation.

Elena: *See you later.*

Cardan: *You can bet on it. Sweet Dreams, Bonita.*

What does that mean?

But I am going to stay with curiosity because I am not going to ask.

CHAPTER EIGHT

After not getting a wink of sleep last night and wandering the orchard with my father all morning, I decide it's time to call Dax. Get it over and done with.

When I give my name to the assistant, I immediately hear her say, "Wait a minute, I'll put you through to Dr. Pearson."

What in the living hell?

"Wow, I was wondering when you'd call," he says in greeting.

"Hello to you too, Dr. Pearson."

"Cut the crap, Elena. I've known you since you were in diapers running around after your brothers."

Oh, the delights of living in a small town. Or near him, in my case.

"Dax, I've decided to take the other tests and see what my options are." There, straight to the point.

I hear him almost sigh in relief. Dax went to school with one of my brothers, so what he said is true, he has known me for a long time.

I hear tapping on the other side of the line as he must be typing something on his computer. I chew on my thumbnail, nasty habit, I know. But when I'm nervous, I can't help it.

"My week is packed, but I can make room for a stress test on Friday at eleven o'clock. I want to start with an ultrasound to check the size of the..."

This isn't looking good.

"You're supposed to keep me from having a heart attack, doctor, not scare the shit out of me," I tell him.

He laughs.

"Do what I tell you, and don't eat anything after seven in the morning. And don't have a big breakfast."

I take out my pad to take notes. This is more complicated than I had imagined.

"Can your father come with you? You are going to need someone to accompany you."

"In case my father can't, Destinee Carr, my friend and a nurse at the hospital, offered to be there."

"Very well, then I'll wait for you here on Friday, and don't make me come looking for you. Clara has taught me a few things."

Now I'm the one laughing. He and his wife make a lovely couple, and their child is a sweetheart.

"I don't doubt it for a moment. I'll see you on Friday, Dax."

Today is Wednesday, and I have the feeling the days until the test will feel like an eternity.

Of course, Cardan Malone will be a welcome distraction.

I sigh with pleasure as I see him walk up the stairs to my porch. Our ranch-style house looks extra inviting with its large wooden frame surrounding it.

Today, instead of bringing lunch like he so frequently does, Mr. Malone carries a clay pot with only two delicate twigs sprouting from its innards.

The butterflies in my stomach come alive at his approach—more than alive, they're practically rioting against each other. Oh, what's the use of lying about it? They ravage me just thinking about him.

"Well, hellooo there!" I say, ignoring the flurry in my chest. "If you didn't bring grub, then I guess you ain't here for no meal?"

He guffaws heartily as he closes the distance between us. "Good to see you, *bonita*!"

My response was meant to be a sly kissy face but becomes a bashful blush after realizing it was far too flirtatious for casual conversation.

"Don't tell me that was an invite for more than just talking?" He eyes me mischievously, and I can barely contain my giddiness. "It doesn't work like that for me. You know that."

Oh gosh, now he's playing hard to get?! Two can play this game, huh, Mr. Malone?

I quip back, "In your dreams!"

His face suddenly darkens as something piques his interest. "In my dreams, Elena… you do way more than just kissing me. Are we going to talk about that now?"

He looks like a dream—dressed in those perfectly worn jeans, a charcoal shirt that clings to his muscular frame, and heavy work boots—as edible as ever.

And those green eyes.

I have never been a huge fan of that color, but….

"If you need someone to listen to your nonsense, there are some good therapists in town, or you may want to call one of those hotlines."

He laughs again. There is something delightfully attractive in a man with a healthy sense of humor and can keep up with mine.

"How about we go out to eat, and I whisper all my naughty dreams to you?"

I bring my hand to my chin, one of my fingers taps the corner of my mouth gently, pretending to think of the invitation. Although I already have the answer on the tip of my tongue.

"Lunch is cheaper than a therapy session…."

"This is for you." He gives me a ceramic pot, ignoring my comment.

"You're doing it wrong, Malone. What happened to chocolates and flowers?"

I take the pot and try to guess what this is about. It's wrapped in clear cellophane and has a little tag folded in half.

"I figured this would be more interesting—and original—than flowers. The girl in the shop told me it's a mystery plant. You must take care of it following the instructions on the card, and in a few weeks, you will receive a surprise."

My curiosity has piqued, so I read the card with the so-called instructions. It is nothing to write home about. Place the pot in indirect light, such as a windowsill and pour some water into it once a day.

I can do that.

And secretly, I must admit I appreciate the creative gift more than just a few flowers. Those die after a few days. This surprise plant is more interesting to me. More Cardan.

"And I suppose you are going to come every day to take care of the plant and see what plant grows?"

He raises his eyebrows, clearly pleased with my answer.

"Of course," he answers. "Now, let's go to lunch. I'm starving, and I have an appointment at the garage at three."

"I don't know, I have things to do at home, and maybe by the time I'm done with them, it will be late. You have an appointment; maybe next time you should call first and give me time to check my schedule."

"Give you time to come up with an excuse? No," he says as he approaches me, so close that I need to tilt my head back to look him in the eye. "Let's have lunch. I promise not to take more than two hours of your time."

In the end, the growl in my stomach tells him what he wants to hear before I can.

Another battle Cardan wins. They say the winner takes it all, my question is, what's the price?

Using GPS, Cardan drives his Jeep to a well-known Italian restaurant here in Sunny Hills. My mother loved this place, which fills me with nostalgia. It isn't pretentious food, simple and with a homemade touch. On weekends, it is impossible to find a free table, but as it is a working day and after the rush hour, the hostess guides us without delay to a booth at the end of the restaurant.

In some weird way, it feels good to come here with Cardan. My father would avoid this place like the plague; too many memories inside these walls. And having someone experience it for the first time, it's like magic.

Cardan makes my heart flutter when he decides to park himself next to me in the booth instead of across the table. I'm sandwiched between the hard wall of his chest and a wooden one. His arm wraps around the back of the chair, trapping me in a tantalizing prison. Taking advantage of my ponytail swept up off my neck, Cardan's lips lightly brush against it, making me shiver with pleasure. His rough beard scrapes against my skin, sending shockwaves throughout my body. The warmth of his breath, followed by the gentle bite of his teeth is too much for me to handle.

"Cardan," I mutter, and it sounds almost like a gasp. "We are in public."

I can feel him laugh before I hear it. "Is that an invitation?"

"No, it's a 'stop' that immediately!" I reprimand him. When he does that, I can't even think straight. "In this town, gossip runs like wildfire, and I don't want it to reach my father that I was here giving a PDA show with you."

A heartbeat, a kiss, and another. "Will you prefer we get takeout?"

Nuh-uh, this isn't a booty call, even though instead of midnight, it is noon.

"You said you have an appointment, and I have work waiting, the payroll…"

"Yes, my meeting…." he murmurs, his tongue wetting my skin. "The first restoration of an old car in my new garage here in Sunny Hills."

I give a little jump of joy in my place, that makes him straighten, but his gaze searches mine, and those little wrinkles appear in the corners of his eyes.

"Tell me more."

This guy should smile more often. I love the way his face lights up with pride. "It's a Camaro 69. It's an iconic vehicle, less than two hundred of these cars are known to still exist."

This is amazing. He's so freaking amazing. A new feeling of pride fills my chest.

"We have to celebrate, so let's eat."

"'I'm looking forward to seeing if it's one of those Mountain Green Metallic; those are a rarity. Restored, one of those could be sold in an auction for more than a million dollars. But I'm talking way too fast. The restoration isn't a fact yet. I haven't inspected the car and duplications…"

My brown eyes are still fixed on his. "It doesn't matter, you only live once. Let's celebrate."

We both are kicking ass. Being awesome.

"What if we go out to dinner tonight? It's not the Saturday I had planned, but we can make it work."

This time I'm not going to refuse.

"Lunch first," I remind him, holding up the menu.

"Lunch first," he repeats, and with that said, he scooches over to look for something on the menu, *my* menu.

When we finish our meal, Cardan takes me back to my house, stopping in front of it, but doesn't get out of the car.

"I'm running late, and I need to print some things before meeting my potential client," he explains. His hand taking mine, firmly since we left the restaurant, our fingers entwined. "I'll pick you up at half-past six, maybe a little earlier."

"It's a date," I finish, approaching him to kiss him on the corner of the mouth. This is just an appetizer; the main dish will arrive in a few hours.

Cardan grabs me by the nape of my neck, keeping our faces close, very close, but not touching.

"See you tonight," he concludes before getting out of the Jeep to open my door.

This man exhibits the utmost gentlemanly behavior, and I'm tickled pink by it.

I spent the day doing my best not to have a mental breakdown over Friday's event. It was much more beneficial to throw myself wholeheartedly into picking out a fetching ensemble for the night and calculating payroll for the week ahead.

The only money we have is from last season's profits, so I need to be savvy about any expenditures. Once our produce is sold, there won't be an influx of cash- just costs like maintaining the trees. Thanks to my father's lawyer, regular deposits are released into my brother's accounts. And when the time comes, the orchard will be mine; they happily agree that this is the best way to keep us together since Papa said he'd seen one too many families fall apart from having no plan whatsoever set in place.

On the bright side, two years ago, we installed a solar energy system which was advised by one of my dad's citrus farm-owning pals. Not only has it done wonders for cutting back on electricity bills, but it also allows us to acquire water at a lower cost to irrigate the orchard.

In hindsight, everything seems quite reasonable and orderly now- so much so that Pops can finally rest easy knowing his children are taken care of.

"All good?" My father asks me after tapping my door frame a couple of times. I left it open, as usual.

"I'm about to finish this month's expenses, payments are ready, and we have some extra money," I look at him and smile, my father has great ideas. Let's see what it's going to be this time. "Last year was good, it allowed us to buy the land and…"

My father sits on the corner of my desk. I must invest in a chair.

"And I want you to invest the money in your future. You could expand the company with that fruit and chili business; you have my full support."

Yes, that sounds great, but to talk about the future, I first have to have answers. Without them, all may be in vain.

"Cardan invited me to dinner tonight," I tell my father. It's not like I'm asking his permission. I'm an adult, and he respects that.

He smiles, although I see some sadness in his eyes. Yes, *papá*, an evil man has come to steal your little girl.

"That doesn't surprise me."

"Well, of course, because you guys were locked in your study for a long time and I'm sure it wasn't to exactly talk about baits and fishing rods," I reply, making fun of him. His intentions were quite obvious, but his heart is in the right place.

"You think you know everything, right?"

"I've known you my whole life," I laugh because that sounded pretty ridiculous. He is my father, of course, he has been with me all my life. He and my mother were expecting another boy and, oh, surprise. I made my entrance into the world, screaming at the top of my lungs. And, ever since then I have been the apple of his eye.

Daddy's little girl. Sugar and spice, and everything nice. Yes, yes, all of that.

There is something else I need to tell him, this is important.

"Could you come with me to see Dax on Friday? He wants me to take some sort of test and…."

"That's soon," he mutters more to himself.

"That's what I said." Which reminds me to order the running shoes. "If you can't go with me, I'll call Dee."

My father looks at me silently for a few seconds, and it makes my stomach clench. I know this is as difficult for him as it is for me. We are a very close family, and for a few weeks in this house that has become too big, it is just him and me.

"I'll be there," and saying this, he comes around my desk and kisses me on the forehead. "*Siempre serás mi niña.*"

Forever my girl.

Oh, *papá*, I wish I had a forever, or at least a long time to offer you, but fate is stealing my future.

♡♡♡

Another thing I must splurge on is some sexy dresses and tops. Nothing but old hoodies, threadbare denims and leggings stuffed in my drawers—perfect for a lazy day here in the orchard, but utterly useless for date nights with a hot man like Cardan.

Thanks to my mother and one of my brother's recent nuptials, I have black, eerily shiny slay-worthy heels that make miracles with my pins, even if they are not exactly new or cutting-edge styles.

Even though Destinee keeps urging me otherwise, nights out just aren't my scene - so imagine the state of my closet outside of office clothes. I scan my wardrobe, trying to find something suitable to impress Cardan wherever he has planned to take me tonight.

I should've asked him beforehand what we were doing. D'oh!

Just as the thought crosses my mind, a call from him appears on my display screen. Huh? He never calls me – like, why do it when texts are much better? I'm sure there's a law about this nowadays or something…

"Elena," I hear him say on the other end of the line. He seems to be out of breath, like he's been running.

"Don't tell me you're on your way, I'm not ready yet." Not even close, I should take a quick bath, do something with my hair…

He sighs loudly. Something tells me unpleasant news are on the way.

"I'm sorry…" There it is, just like I thought. "Right now, I'm on my way to Los Angeles. The last flight has already left, so I'll have to take a road trip."

That is not a short drive to do in one day.

His image appears in my mind, him, driving his Jeep with one hand while running the fingers of the other through the thick strands of his dark blond hair.

The tone of his voice makes it clear to me that he's worried, something must have happened.

"Is everything okay?" Stupid question, I know, but I don't know how else to ask without sounding too nosy or worse, gossipy.

"I don't know," he sighs. "A problem with one of my administrators at the Long Beach shop. I suppose I'll find out in the morning after the meeting."

"You're going to be tired." I blurt out before I know it.

He lets out a small laugh, and a smile pulls at my lips. It comforts me to know that I have lightened the moment even a little.

"I guess tomorrow I'm going to need the help of my old friend Joe," he answers. "Don't worry; it's not the first time something like this has happened."

I guess not, but it's the first time since we've been together.

Are we together?

Oh, the nonsense that comes to my mind...

"When are you coming back?" I hate that my voice sounds so whiny.

"Do you miss me already?" Arrogant man, I can almost see him smile from my window. "If it's any consolation, I'm going to be thinking about you the whole time," he adds. "How about you send me a picture of your boobs to keep me company in the meantime?"

He's joking. He has to be. We haven't reached that point in our relationship. In fact, he has not seen them in person, not once.

And yet, I find myself staring at the bra I'm wearing. Will I ever have the courage to do it? Not that I have much to show him either, I barely fill a B cup.

"Is your mind always in the gutter?"

"Always," he laughs again. The deep hoarse sound makes my nipples harden. Holy mother, just imagining what happened this afternoon in the restaurant when he put his lips on my skin, I shudder. I don't know where this might lead. But it is a fact that we will soon forget about clothes.

"Perv."

"I won't touch you unless you give me permission," he replies. "But my imagination has no bounds, *Bonita.*"

"I want you to touch me," I assure him with a gasp. "All over."

My heart beats faster as I hear him release another long breath. "An erection on Interstate 5, this is torture."

"You started the game," I remind him.

"And you, Elena, have given me another reason to return as soon as possible," he says. "I'll call you in the morning. Dream of me."

CHAPTER NINE

I never thought my heart could shatter into a million pieces like a mirror. I mean, come on! That kind of thing only happens in romance novels, right? But lately, I feel like the heroine of one of those stories; all I think about is that tattooed bad boy who's got me going crazy. Me, the manager of a freaking mango orchard. Who has time for love and nonsense when there are literally tons of fruit to cultivate?

But no matter how tired I am at night; I can't seem to fall asleep. So I come up with a brilliant idea:

Google it! Turns out, there are clinical studies and treatments galore...none of which make any sense to me. So I try something else: 'live with' and 'patient with'.

Who knew forums existed where people posted their sob stories and horror-show experiences? But after reading through them all, I realize one thing. This isn't my time yet.

Feeling blue, I spend all morning in my bed, thinking hard. Why? What for?

It's past noon, and the pity party is in full swing when Destinee comes and pulls me out of my safety cocoon.

Ah, my best friend and her timing...

"Hurry, we're going to Napa right now, we have a reservation for a five o'clock tour of the vineyard, and we don't want to miss it. Pick up your things; we're leaving!"

I stare at her for a few minutes as she balances on the balls of her feet. She looks like a little girl and is certainly acting like one.

I don't want to go, I want to stay here in my room and write my bucket list, which I should have done weeks ago, but as they say, better late than never, right?

"I have things to do Dee; you told me we were going tomorrow."

"Ha! You look very busy indeed. Get up. It's Friday, so get your bag. Adventure awaits us." She moves her arms to emphasize her words like she's turned into a fairy or something like that.

For a couple of seconds, I stare at her in silence, my friend may be missing a couple of screws, but she's right about something. Adventure is waiting, and I may not have to go swimming with sharks to make every second count.

Have some fun to get me out of this rut. Enjoy a few glasses of wine, each step is a step forward. And well, better Napa than the walls of my room; any distraction is welcome, after all.

I don't want to spend my time crying or wallowing in misery. Fate has already stolen enough from me.

From the evil gleam that twinkles in her eyes, I can tell that she has noticed my change in attitude, so I put my bored expression back on and try to make my voice sound flat by saying, "I need at least twenty minutes to pack my suitcase, wait for me in the kitchen."

Destinee has never waited for me in the kitchen while I prepare to go out for the weekend with her. I have always packed while she settled in my bed and judged each one of my choices.

This is definitely a first time, but as I said, it's all part of the show. I don't want to be extra excited about this.

Although I recognize that it is very welcome.

"Don't worry about anything," I hear my father say. "Just have fun."

Have fun. This is just a distraction, not a long-term solution. The future worthy of a Hallmark card that I longed for all my life is left behind. The letters I wrote were lost at sea; damn the universe has once again managed to conspire against me. But as long as I am here, I hope to enjoy it to the best of my ability. And that means feeling good.

Although that shadow is always there, hovering over me like a black cloud.

Five minutes under the warm running water helps me plan what to pack. The clothes I planned to wear to date Cardan, my smuttiest underwear, even when it's just for me now. A bikini, another outfit to go out to dinner tomorrow night, what little makeup I have in a little bag, my shoes, and I'm done.

I can pack like a Girl Scout. When I want to, of course.

Half an hour later, as I walk down the hall that leads to the kitchen, I can hear my father and Destinee chatting. I'm sure of what they're talking about since they've both done a very poor job of hiding it. My suspicions are confirmed when realizing that I've entered the kitchen, my father clears his throat, and Dee changes the subject to absurdity.

"Has the kitchen been painted since the last time I was here?" she asks, looking at the light green walls as if it were the first time she had seen them.

"What are you doing wasting time?" I claim. "Let's go now."

I see my father walk away down the same corridor that I just walked through with a satisfied expression, this was his idea, of course, it was.

I love you too, papá, but right now I'm not going to agree with you.

Between my father and my best friend, I have been ambushed.

Well, here we go, play along. I have nothing to lose, and it seems like I have a lot more to gain.

No more than ten minutes have passed in silence when Dee begins the conversation. The topic can't be any other than Cardan Malone.

"So what are you going to do with him?" she asks me, straight to the point.

"I don't know," the truth is my head is busy with matters of the heart, and not exactly figuratively. "First, I'm going to wait for him to return from his trip, and then... I know he is attracted to me, but exactly what he wants, I don't know."

She takes her gaze off the road for a couple of seconds, just long enough to look at me and roll her eyes.

"That man is so freaking hot. Like panty-melting hot. If you don't want him, I'll offer myself as a tribute and let the lust games begin."

That statement gives me a stab of jealousy that I've never felt in my chest before. This attraction thing is starting to turn into something else. I like Cardan. I can't deny it.

"Hey, I want him for myself!" I protest.

"Oh yeah, did you call dibs already?" She asks me, looking at me for a couple of beats. "Did you lick him? Otherwise, I still have my chance."

That makes me laugh. I can imagine her as a kitten sticking her tongue out... and again jealousy. The Medusa that is taking over me has forgotten that Destinee is my best friend and that she would not get between Cardan and me. I trust Dee, I know she wouldn't.

And speaking of licks, the memory of his mouth sliding over my neck, making me vibrate. A chill runs through my whole body... the next time I see him, maybe things between us will go a step further.

Next time I see him, when will that be? He said he hoped to return today, but he hasn't sent me a message and it is past noon.

Could it be that he has been driving back or that his business in Los Angeles has become more complicated than he expected?

Gah, Elena, stop justifying his disappearance. When a boy disappears for no apparent reason, it can only mean one thing. And the message is clear. He isn't into you.

It appears that Cardan Malone turned out to be much ado about nothing.

After that, Dee changes the subject to local gossip because my friend finds out about everything. How she does it, that's been a mystery since we were in school.

A few minutes later, Destinee stops the car in front of a hotel, which isn't where we usually stay when we come to Napa.

This is way out of our budget.

"Have you gone crazy?" I yell at her, not even daring to open the car door. "What are we doing here?"

She looks at me, a triumphant smile on her lips.

"I had some help," she acknowledges with a shrug. Yes, my father definitely got a hand in this; there's no other way Destinee could afford this without making a big hole in her monthly budget. She makes good money working at the hospital, but not *this* good.

Staying at a five-star luxury hotel is not normal—we are more of the bargain and outlet store kind of girls.

"Don't worry; we are going to enjoy the weekend without being bothered." I look at her and open my mouth to protest, but she raises her hand, stopping my words. "I got a good deal, it is low season, and they needed to fill up the hotel, so the price was amazing."

She winks at me and turns to hand over the keys to her cherry red Corolla to the valet, who is waiting with a gloved hand, ready to take over our transportation.

The hotel, from the outside, is an imposing stone façade partially covered by ivy, which at this time of year is not that green, but the result is still beautiful.

I follow my best friend across the marble floor of the lobby and wait, staring at the wood-beamed ceiling as she takes over the registration desk.

Dee opens the door to the hotel room to reveal walls painted in a creamy eggshell hue. Two plush queen beds are pushed up against each other, and there is a window that opens out onto a small balcony with views of the glimmering river. A wave of appreciation washes over me as I realize how much Dee has gone through to get us this incredible deal—but it feels a little too luxurious for my current situation.

It's after five in the afternoon, so I imagine that the spa day will have to wait until tomorrow.

"What's the plan?" I ask her from the balcony because I'm so excited that I don't know what to do with myself.

"Change your clothes because in a few minutes, our hot yoga class starts, and after that, we'll have enough time to change for dinner in one of the tasting rooms."

"You, liar. You said we had an appointment for a vineyard tour." My index is pointing at her, this isn't that we talked about. "Destinee, I came here to relax and have a good time. You know exercising isn't my thing."

She gazes at me with the typical school principal expression of pity and reprimand. I could feel my inner child squirm in meekness. We stood in our spandex, ready to rent two yoga mats from the gym entrance.

"This is going to be epic!" she proclaimed, almost convincing me.

Yoga time, they said. Fun times, they said. Alas, my flexibility was as stiff as wood. I couldn't keep up with the teacher's commands except for maybe the Child's Pose - sometimes it was hard to tell if I was doing that right too.

The instructor announced this class was for beginners. But everyone in the room had their own level of expertise; even Destinee seemed to have no problem following along. While I felt like a contorted knot most the time.

The easy part? Racing out of there like a bat due to a heated competition against my friend over who can get first access to the bathroom shower. She spent quite some money on this swanky hotel, so sharing a room was inevitable...but winning first dibs on this particular victory is already worth its weight in gold.

"What time is our dinner reservation?" I ask Destinee as I fasten the necklace that I have decided to wear tonight.

Since my wardrobe department's options are limited, I wore what I had found in my closet for my failed date with Cardan. High-waisted jeans, my highest heels, a long-sleeved black bodysuit that reveals my shoulders and the upper part of my neckline. Also, I have dried my dark hair in soft waves that go down my back.

I look at myself in the full-length mirror and inwardly give myself two thumbs up. I look hot.

No one could say that I am a girl who walks through life with a broken heart.

I carry that secret hidden inside me. Literally.

"Here, put this on," says Dee giving me a gentle nudge on the shoulder, in her outstretched hand is a little tube of deep red lipstick. The color is gorgeous, but I'm not used to wearing a bold color like that.

"That's not my jam," I start to protest, but again she stops me with her eyes.

"What happened with being more adventurous? Come on, live a little."

That's true, and well, no one was ever hurt wearing Chanel red lips.

We are on our way five minutes later. We have a reservation, after all.

"Shit, I left my phone in the room," Dee grumbled when we've gone down to the hotel lobby, ready—and hungry. "Go ahead to the restaurant. I don't want to miss the reservation."

She heads back to the elevator, and I stand there, thinking that I'm pretty sure I saw her put her cell phone in her little handbag a while ago, but she walks away so fast that I don't have time to tell her.

I walk to the restaurant. When I get there, I give my friend's name to the hostess and she, smiling, welcomes me and then leads me to a table in the corner of the terrace.

It is very beautiful here; the atmosphere is romantic and intimate. This is not what I expected when Dee spoke of fun. This calls for something else. As I sit, a sense of longing takes hold in my chest that I have never experienced before.

I would like to be here sharing this with someone else. Someone who would take my hand across the table, and while looking into my eyes, could see in his, the reflection of my own soul.

I look at the candle in the center of the table and then beyond the stone railing, the river is softly illuminated by small lights masterfully set on the shore. This is definitely precious.

The perfect place for a romantic date.

The chair on the other side of the table sounds like when someone moves it across the floor.

"Did you find your phone?" I ask, looking up, hoping to find Destinee ready for dinner.

The truth is that I'm starving.

But my friend isn't six feet tall, nor does she have a beard, nor a body carved out of stone.

Nor is she the owner of those green eyes that look at me, knowing that the game's winning point has been scored.

Well, if his intention was to surprise me, he succeeded. Home run.

"Good evening, *Bonita,*" he greets me with a sideways smile.

"What are you doing here?"

CHAPTER TEN

"Surprise," he says without shame or remorse.

Surprise, indeed.

Cheeky, sure, this wasn't a coincidence.

"What are you doing here?" I question. I want answers, and I want them right now.

"I'm going to have dinner, and I hope you do too," he responds, looking all smug.

I look at him for a moment, narrowing my eyes. Yes, I can deny it all I want, but the fact that he is here, that he prepared this ambush, I like it. I like it very much.

And I like you too, Cardan Malone.

Even I'm surprised to hear those words echo in my head. This isn't fling material. If I let Cardan in, it will be like the fall of Troy. Serious, serious consequences.

Cardan picks up the menu and hums a little song while he reads it.

"Do you want me to order for you?" he asks me with those lips still curled up. But I don't take my eyes off him. The view is much better than the menu.

And boy, does the man look edible, I know he's wearing jeans, I noticed it as he was sitting down. He is also wearing a black shirt and a black leather jacket, the kind that motorcyclists wear. His beard is slightly trimmed, and his hair has been slicked back.

"I can do it myself, thank you very much." A note of sarcasm is evident in my voice, but this time I can't avoid the smile painted on my face.

The menu consists of simple food made fancy, pizza, fried chicken, artisan pasta... and that is precisely what catches my attention.

"Ready to order?" Cardan asks me, and as soon as I nod, he calls the waiter.

A bottle of red wine from the hotel's winery appears on our table a few minutes later. I know very little about wine, but I know what I like and what I don't. And this is very good.

"I thought you were still in Los Angeles," I tell him after taking a short sip from my drink.

He smiles, leaning over the table a little, his forearms on the white tablecloth; what a distraction.

"The plan was always to come back today. Fortunately, I was able to fix the incident before it turned worse. My shop is in good hands, and everything is back to normal."

He says it so calmly that it is easy to believe him.

"What happened?" Curiosity killed the cat, they say.

"Competition..." he sighs. "One of my branch managers was accepting money from another chain to pass him information on a contract that we are about to sign with a trucking agency. It's nothing to write home about, maintenance and stuff, but money keeps my payroll up to date. No one can afford to lose customers these days."

That's the truth, thankfully, I've never had to deal with that kind of foul play, but sometimes negotiations can get ugly. Luckily my father, being a pretty tough negotiator, taught me well.

"I understand," I tell him sincerely.

"My lawyers are handling everything now." He ends those words with a heavy sigh. "But you know what? I've been driving for six hours straight, and I've been anticipating this for several days, so the last thing I want is to talk about my work issues."

In a rather poor attempt to hide my smile, I take the glass in my hand before leaning back and searching his eyes with mine.

"So, what do you wanna talk about?"

He leans forward more, which makes him look bigger. More intimidating. "I want you to tell me what you did while I was away."

"I've decided on my next adventure," I tell him, and he raises his eyebrows.

"Am I going to have to buy a wetsuit and diving equipment?"

That makes me laugh. This man never ceases to amaze me. Talking to him is so easy.

"For what?"

"To swim with sharks," he replies. "Isn't that next on your crazy adventure list?"

I laugh, remembering one of our first conversations.

"No, actually, I've thought it through, and I'm not sure that's my thing," I confess, being completely honest. "But a tattoo does sound like a great idea."

He smiles, and I see something shining in his eyes which I've never seen before.

"You know they are addictive, right?" he tells me. "I have a few, and I see more in my future."

"What? You took a fortune teller course while you were away?" I can't help but tease him a bit.

"Wait until you see the ink on your skin." As he utters those words, he puts his fingers to his mouth. My eyes follow the path they trace on his lips, his mouth is so tempting. The memory of his warm lips on my neck. My mind travels and begins to imagine hundreds of scenarios where we are alone, and clothes aren't necessary. "I'm also dying to see it... to..."

Cardan doesn't need to finish that sentence. In the silence, I can hear his voice, loud and clear. I want that, too, even though I know this is only going to lead to disaster. This is an adventure I can't embark on, not only for myself but also for him.

What can I offer him? Cardan is a man seeking a future, and I'm not sure that's in my cards.

One year? Maybe two?

And then what? When he realizes that there isn't more than that, we'll be embroiled in a tragedy that could have been avoided.

If it were so easy.

If he wasn't so determined.

So insistent.

Cardan clears his throat and settles in his chair before asking, "Do you know what tattoo you want?"

"The beat of a hea..." I reply without adding the second part. The beat of a healthy heart. Not a broken one, like mine.

"Because of your mother, right?" Damn man and the town where you can get the family history with photocopies, photos, and everything. Why can't people keep stuff to themselves?

"Yes," I say without delving into the subject. There is much more than that; everything was unleashed when she left.

He must know that this topic is off-limits for me, a wound that still festers.

Just then, our dinner arrives, and my mouth starts to water at the sight of it. My stomach demands sustenance after that yoga class Dee made me endure. A delicious tomahawk steak with a baked potato and salad sound far more appealing than a chicken breast with boiled vegetables.

This could be one of the last times I can afford such extravagance, so I'm going to fully enjoy every bite. As I sink my teeth into the juicy meat, I emit an involuntary groan of delight, and Cardan laughs heartily, dabbing his mouth with his napkin.

"Now," I tell him after swallowing. "How did you organize all this? And where do you know Destinee from?"

He takes a sip of his wine before replying: "Those are a lot of questions for a single sentence."

"And you are going to answer them all."

"A magician never reveals his tricks, *Bonita*."

"You aren't a wizard," I reply with a hint of sassiness. "You are a mechanic, and right now, you are going to spill the beans."

"When you told me you had plans for the weekend, you piqued my curiosity," he confesses hoarsely. "So I decided to find out what was so important that it was getting in my way."

Determination, another ingredient to add to this dangerous combination that is Cardan Malone.

Why is life sending me the perfect man at the most imperfect moment?

"And how did you find Destinee?" I insist.

He lets out a soft laugh before answering me. "Your English teacher, Mrs. Richards, was in the garage the other day. Did you know that the transmission of her Mercedes S65 AMG has been giving her trouble? That gave us a couple of minutes to talk."

I can imagine it, and if, by chance, Cardan offered her a cupcake, I'm sure my old teacher must have even mentioned my brothers' antics. That woman has a better memory than an elephant and a lot of time to spare.

"Finding Destinee at the hospital wasn't difficult," he ends with a shrug.

But there is one point that remains pending.

"When did you have time to do all this? Weren't you out of town trying to solve the mess with your business?"

He smiles as if the gesture contains all the answers I want to hear.

"Never doubt a man's determination, Elena," he murmurs while his gaze stays glued to mine. "Nobody deserves something they aren't willing to fight for."

His words give me goosebumps. He has no idea what he does to me. Cardan not only makes me feel, but he also makes me think.

Dammit.

"How is it that any smart woman has caught you?" It's incredible. He's a catch, that's for sure. "Any girl would be happy to call you her own."

"I'm not an easy colt to catch," he tells me. The electricity is here, sizzling in our midst. It is tangible. "Nor meek to ride."

The double meaning doesn't escape me. What would I give to see it—just a taste?

The problem? I know it won't be enough. With him, it would just be the beginning.

"How's everything?" The waiter asks, cutting off our exchange.

"Great, thanks," Cardan replies without taking his eyes off me.

His gaze strips me and, at the same time, makes me feel safe. It is a unique combination like everything about him.

"Tell me." Trying to change the topic of this conversation to something less compromising. "Did you have time to see your family?"

There it is, safe ground.

Cardan looks down at his French fries before putting one in his mouth, chewing it before answering me.

"I'm my mom's only child. She and her husband invited me to dinner at their house. I saw them, and they're doing well.

Dick is good to her, that makes me happy, and knowing that she isn't alone gives me the freedom to live my life."

I come from a Latino family roots are important to us. If he were a jerk to his mother, that would knock him out of the picture immediately. And I also understand what he means. My father is alone now, and I can't just leave him now that my brothers have made their lives out of town. I feel a little responsible for him.

"So you went into the wolf's den, did there happen to be a pretty blonde girl, one of her friend's daughters, dining with you that night?"

We both laughed at my bad joke. My brothers left before my mother had a chance to do something like that, but I've heard some horror stories.

"I told her that a girl with a smart mouth has caught my eye," he says quietly, like someone who is confessing a secret, I look at him with wide eyes. "I also told her that this beautiful brunette is making the hunt quite difficult for me."

I bring my wine glass to my lips, which gives me a couple of seconds to think about how to answer. Then I remember his words.

"Nobody deserves something they aren't willing to fight for," I tell him, turning the tables.

He looks at me with darkened eyes. Now those deep irises look almost the color of emeralds. I find myself mesmerized by them.

"Smart words, *Bonita,*" he murmurs, his eyes fixed on mine. "Well played."

We finish the meal slowly, by the time our plates are clean, most of the other patrons have left. The air has turned cold, but my skin has prickled for a very different reason.

"Do you want to walk for a bit?" I ask him after he takes care of the bill as we walk down the cobblestone terrace.

He says nothing as we take a couple of steps in silence.

"Unless you're tired… with the trip and all that…"

Why this sudden shyness? I am not normally like this.

Cardan takes my hand before answering and lifting it makes me turn like we were in the middle of a dance floor. My hair flies and I laugh like a fool.

"I'm always up for a stroll," he smiles. I want to put my hands on that chest covered by the cotton of his shirt and the leather of his jacket.

This man does things to me, and I'm feeling them right now.

All of them.

My hand is still in his as we walk along the riverbank. Which seems perfect, our fingers intertwined, the touch is intimate. It's not like those guys who hold hands by cupping your hand, which reminds me that Cardan Malone isn't a boy. He is a man.

And he knows what he wants.

Me.

There are a few trees. As we pass under them, their shadows are my friends. I take refuge in them to hide. To stop my racing heart that wants to follow what it feels.

Cardan grabs me by the waist, pulling my body to his. He takes my chin in his hands and his lips crash against mine. A spark of electricity races through my veins at the knowledge that I'm in his arms again. His tongue slides against mine, slowly and passionately as

I let out a soft moan.

My hands trail up his chest before they wrap around the back of his neck, locking us in an embrace. Our chests press together, and I can feel the heat radiating from him, while he tenderly caresses my face with one hand. His other hand wander down my body as I fist his shirt with desire filled intensity.

The kiss intensifies as he lifts me off the ground and carries me away into paradise. Our chests are so close that I can feel the beating of his heart beating as fast as mine. I fist his shirt with my hands, arching my back, seeking more closeness. The top I'm wearing leaves a lot of skin exposed. But right now, it's getting in the way.

My whole being vibrates like the string of a bow after shooting the arrow. So much that I think I'm about to break. And with that my will.

Kissing him was a mistake. A big one.

"This doesn't mean I'm going to sleep with you tonight," I tell him when I've caught my breath, placing my palms on his chest to push him gently.

Where did I get the determination to say those words? I don't know myself.

Cardan's forehead rests on mine, his breath warm on my lips, as he says, "That is your decision, and I will respect it. You don't have to do anything. I can wait, but that doesn't mean I can't sneak into your dreams."

Does he have six toes? This man can't be that perfect.

He must have some flaw. Anything. Something.

CHAPTER ELEVEN

"You're definitely dumb," Dee chides me as Pia—the masseuse—hits a knot of tension, making me moan. "You should have gone to bed with the man, and I was counting on that. Hoping to enjoy the room to myself for the weekend and stuff…"

Pia is still doing magic with her fingers, she is excellent, and I need some relaxation. Maybe every adventure doesn't have to be filled with adrenaline; just doing something for myself is enough. Something that I like, that fills me up.

"Remind me why I'm still talking to you…"

Destinee has the nerve to laugh.

"Because I'm the bestest friend you could get in this vast world," she praises herself. "Who else was going to plan this luxury hotel weekend getaway for you?"

I close my eyes for a moment, enjoying the massage they are giving me on my lower back. Now I know why she has been able to afford this type of accommodation and everything else. Not forgetting to include this massage, everything has come from Mr. Malone's credit card in a Cinderella style. Only in my case, the fairy godmother is a girl who is missing a couple of wires in that head of hers and believes that being with Cardan will fill a void.

"Dee, as nice as this is, you can't be doing things like this behind my back. It's crazy."

I can't see her face from where I am, but I'm sure she's rolling her eyes. Hard.

"How else is a surprise supposed to be planned?" Her question is full of sarcasm. "I didn't receive the memo reminding me of the authorized list of things that I can plan as a surprise."

This conversation is ridiculous because this whole situation is too.

"I'm going to have to talk to him, you know?" I say after a few minutes of silence. "I have to make it clear to him that even though I appreciate all this, I'm not the girl he is looking for."

I hear Destinee mutter something to the masseuse and then the sound of her stretching as she rises to face me. Yes, even with my head tucked into the hole in the massage bed, I can see it.

"Don't start with that nonsense about what you are going through. Talk to Malone, tell him what's wrong with you, your diagnosis, and that's it." Oh yes, as if it were so easy. "Look at your parents. our mother lived happily for many years without knowing what was happening, if she had known…"

I know, but it also happens that although physically we are very similar, my mother and I don't think the same. We are very different people. Or we were, I don't know anymore.

"And now look at my father; he's alone, Dee. Alone."

My throat tightens at the thought of that, the heart attack, and everything that happened afterward. The deep pain in which my father is in, my brothers—all of us.

I couldn't do that to another family, to a man I loved with all my heart.

Much less pass the death sentence to my children. It isn't a possibility that I would even dare to consider. It would be unfair, tremendously unfair.

And I know because that's how I feel.

"That's a decision you can't make on your own, Lena," she insists, this time putting her hand on my shoulder. "Talk to Cardan. If he runs away, at least we will have enjoyed this weekend. But maybe he'll stay… Besides, the guy is better than the mangoes in your orchard, and you know very well that I am a fan of your mangoes. Take a bite out of this one, I bet his chili is spicy, too."

Only my friend can make me laugh at a time like this.

I close my eyes, and for a moment, I dare to dream, just for a moment. And later…

"No, Dee, this is impossible."

"Lena, you told me yourself that Cardan is a man, and he knows what he wants," she insists. "For some reason, it has gotten into his head that that's you, talk to him. Give him a chance to decide. Give yourself a chance, too, you are more than a heart condition."

This time I am the one who gets up from the table. I murmur an apology to Pia, and with tears in my eyes as I go to look for my clothes. I need to get out of here. I need to go home.

In the elevator on the way up to our room, I have to breathe, but unfortunately, I'm not alone. Two more couples have sneaked into the metal box. I breathe as I look at the ceiling, trying to calm myself, silently as king, whoever rules this universe to give me the strength to get out of this mess.

Mom, help me. I need you.

If she were here, she would know what to do. Eventually, we would be on the same page.

Just as I'm about to slide the card to unlock the door to our hotel room, my phone chimes, announcing the arrival of a new text message.

It's him. Of course, it is.

Cardan: I'm sitting by the pool, and it's too quiet without you here.

I take a deep breath, a vain attempt to calm my heart that threatens to jump out of my chest every time I think of him. This is why a relationship, even a weekend one with him would be dangerous.

My heart is broken. But I'm going to learn to live with it.

With a devastated heart, I don't know if I would survive.

♡♡♡

It doesn't take long to find the man, who indeed, is sneaking into my dreams.

Cardan Malone, shirtless, is a sight to behold. And, as an art lover, I take a moment to admire him, taking advantage of the fact that he hasn't realized that I am here.

Too hot to handle. The man is like one of those marble sculptures in the famous museums around the world. "My body reacts in a rush of lust.

He isn't lying on one of the chairs, he is walking with his back to me and talking on the phone. His hair is dry, which means he hasn't gone into the pool. My eyes follow the strong lines of the perfect triangle on his back to the waistband of his navy trunks that hangs from his slim hips, the black ink of a tattoo accentuating them from shoulder to upper arm and shoulder blade. My fingers itch to trace those edges, to run them in with my mouth.

My mind is wandering, and I just arrived.

Cardan turns around like he knows I'm standing here ogling him. He smirks, and, I am surprised to realize how strange it's not to see the sparkle in his eyes because now they are covered by those classic sunglasses.

I walk over, and he does the same, cutting the distance that separates us.

"We'll talk later, Nic," he tells whoever is on the other side of the phone before ending the call.

His eyes roam over me from head to toe without dissimulation; no, I'm not dressed in a particular way: some black leggings, a white T-shirt, and a long wine-colored cardigan. The sun is shining on us, making this day strangely warm for this time of year. How he endures the weather with so little clothing is a mystery, one worthy of being grateful. It's not every day that a girl gets the chance to see something like this.

When we're so close that my chucks clad feet are facing his bare feet, he kisses my cheek. His beard scrapes my skin, awakens the memory of our kiss. I can still feel it on my lips.

"Are you hungry?" He asks me at the same time that a few words come out of my mouth. "We have to talk."

He looks at me; his eyes are still covered by those sunglasses, which at this moment seems to annoy me.

"Ok, let's order something to eat first, then we can talk all you want."

After ordering a charcuterie board and a bottle of white wine—because hey, we're in Napa, we've come to drink—I drop into one of the lounge chairs, and Cardan sits next to me, putting on a sweatshirt. He sits so close that our bodies are touching.

I don't know what this means, but my heart is about to jump out of my chest, and it's hard for me to breathe.

God, I'm going to have a heart attack right here.

"What do you want to talk about?" he asks me, realizing that no words have left my lips after a long beat of silence.

"What do you want from me?" There it is, straight to the point.

"Isn't it clear?" he murmurs, turning his body to face me. I am unable to do the same; my eyes are fixed on the water in the empty pool in front of us. "I'm on the verge of falling in love with you, Elena."

What? Did he just say that he is downhill with no breaks for me?

"But you don't know me," I answer, raising my voice. I think my brain just short-circuited.

"That's easy to fix," he counters, his gaze looking for mine.

"That takes time," I tell him. "And that is something I can't offer you."

One of his big hands runs down his beard making me wonder how would it feel against my skin. He doesn't play fair. "Elena, I *am* a busy man with a business to run. I'm not the demanding or needy type if I've given you that impression..."

No, no, this conversation is getting off track.

"This is the true case of, it's not you, it's me, Cardan."

"Famous words," he responds, looking at the same place as me.

"Listen, there's one thing I'm sure of, and it's that I can't put my heart into a relationship right now," I whisper. "But if what you want is a good time and a good time in bed, I'm your girl."

It's getting a little cold, but I can feel a bead of sweat coming down my back, and my heart leaps so fast in my chest that I swear it's about to spill down my throat.

Cardan has gone silent, surely in shock upon hearing my words.

"A good lay," I hear him mutter.

It seems like a cloud has come down from the sky, making this moment tense. Heavy.

"Don't you dare judge me. If it's alright for a boy to tell a girl that a relationship is not part of the picture, then why should I be judged and sentenced to with a scarlet letter over my chest? This is what I have to offer, Cardan, the only thing I have to offer you."

He looks like I've struck him so hard all the air has left his lungs.

"I'm sorry, I didn't mean to offend you, I swear it was not my intention, but it's just…"

"Is that what you want?"

I am unable to form a coherent answer. Of course, this isn't what I had dreamed of. Who am I kidding? I was the girl who made her mother drive her to the Pier in San Francisco to drop letters into a bottle on Valentine's Day.

No girl dreams that her story has the minutes counted.

"So all you want is for me to fuck you?" he says, breaking the silence, like he still doesn't believe my statement.

"Well, there is no need to say it in such a crass way, but yeah. I mean, we just met, you're new to town and all that. I know you have a business to manage and a thousand things to do on a daily basis, so do I. I'm just easing the way for you."

I look at him, hating the glasses he's wearing. I can't see his eyes, and I don't like that. Many times those green depths say more than his words.

"Frankly, I think the best thing for you right now is something other than sex."

I want to take off his glasses, but that movement would imply intimacy and trust, and that is a bridge that I do not want to cross between us.

This is a cold operation, like that of a surgeon. Mechanics. Yeah, yeah, I know we're talking about naked bodies and all that. But you can separate sex from the heart, right?

Many people do.

"Who hurt you, *Bonita*?" he asks me, turning to look at me. Finally, he takes off his glasses, and my breath catches in my throat.

The green of his emerald irises glisten in the sunlight, my heart rate is racing, and this time, I can't blame the thickened muscles.

He is absolutely perfect.

A weight is installed in my chest when I see the hurt in his eyes; that wounded me too. If only he knew how deep my wound is.

If only I could tell him the truth…

How do I convince him that this is what I want when I am not sure myself?

An adventure, the adventure of my life.

"And won't I be able to convince you to take the leap with me?"

One of his hands rests on my cheek, his rough thumb almost caressing my mouth. Somehow, I manage to smile, even though I don't feel like it.

I'm about to do something very stupid, like leave him or let him kiss me.

And that can't happen.

At least not now.

"I'm sorry, Cardan. I know I'm being an idiot."

He shakes his head before speaking. "You aren't an idiot. You are just a wounded bird, and you are afraid." He sighs and continues. "My life is complicated, it's true, I haven't decided what to do with my future yet, but I think I am ready for something more permanent than a one-night stand."

His eyes search mine, my damn lungs still not wanting to function properly.

"You want more, and you want it with me. How can you be so sure? We just met a couple of weeks ago."

He lets out a breath that feels warm on my skin.

"We're going to do whatever you want," he tells me, and I swear I want to dance with relief. I'm ready to drop my list of rules for him when he continues. "But on the condition that you agree to give me a chance."

I look at him with wide eyes. Can we make this work without expecting anything beyond the day-to-day?

"Cardan…" I speak his name, almost begging him to let this go.

There's no future. There isn't.

You only live once, and I can't steal his life in the same way that fate has stolen mine.

That's the truth. I am fated.

"You are what every girl dreams of having."

"But not you," he adds.

"At another time, me too. A few months ago, I would accept without hesitation. But the truth is that now I just want to have fun, enjoy the moment. I know that may seem selfish to many people, but it's the truth. Time flies, and I…"

He looks at me for a moment, studying me.

"This has to do with your mother's death, I understand."

"Yes, it does have to do with that," I tell only half-truth. "I want to live, Cardan, I want to find myself. I want to discover what makes me vibrate; what makes my heart race."

"And you want me to be part of your adventure." His voice serious as his stern face.

Yes, that's exactly what I'm looking for. Passion. Adrenaline.

I look into his eyes, silently begging him to accept my proposal. Cardan is older than me. The confidence with which he moves speaks of experience, experience that I lack. He holds the key to open the cage door. The key to my sexual freedom.

"I want this to be good for you, Elena. I want to give you what you want, think about you offering this to the next guy who crosses your path, and he says yes. Because a man has to be an idiot to reject a beauty like you," he says, and I want to jump with pleasure. "But my condition remains the same."

One of his hands goes down my neck until he takes me by the base. Our eyes still do not detach, and we remain dangerously close. We are only a couple of inches apart.

"I don't want to waste time on false expectations, jealousy, and pointless fighting, Cardan."

Time is precious, and it doesn't come back. I can't buy it either like in that Justin Timberlake movie. That's the reason they call the present a gift.

"I'm not going to share you with anyone." As he says it, his fingers on the back of my neck tighten. I gasp in surprise at how good it feels.

"Neither do I," I add. Surely the female population of Sunny Hills will not agree with this, but for the duration of this agreement, if I agree to be with him, Cardan Malone will be mine and only mine.

"I'm fighting for you, Elena." He surprises me with that bold statement. "One chance, that's all I need, only one. I won't waste it."

I don't have the strength to say no, not when we're like this. When he has me like this.

And the words don't come out of my throat, so I nod. The gesture is slight, almost imperceptible, but I know that he's noticed because in his eyes triumph shines.

He knows he has gotten his way.

"Come with me," he says, getting up and holding out his hand, waiting for mine.

My mind has gone blank. A flat line.

I've got what I'm looking for, why the heck doesn't it feel quite right?

CHAPTER TWELVE

This is happening. Right now.

Cardan leads me by the hand through the extensive courtyard of the hotel; instead of heading inside, we go to the far side of the property. There, hidden among the trees, is a small stone house. A couple of minutes later, he is closing the door behind me.

Literally.

"Elena…" he says my name, his gaze on mine. Those green eyes that I like so much are full of emotions that scare me.

And what terrifies me the most is to think what he can see in mine.

My body has ceased to belong to me. When all his hard anatomy presses against mine, trapping me against the door, I know I am lost.

In more ways than one.

This is a bad idea.

This is the best idea I've ever had.

He puts his hand back on the nape of my neck and pulls me so that our lips meet. Correction, our mouths don't meet. They collide.

A soft moan escapes from my mouth, we have kissed very few times, but its taste is something I want to savor with my tongue forever. I've never tasted anything like this before. I've never been kissed like this before.

I bet that tongue can do magic, that makes an electric current go straight through me.

A low growl that begins in his chest makes lust roar through my veins, and when it leaves his lips something erupts inside me. What I feel for him is not desire. It is necessity.

I don't even want to think about how many women touched his lips before mine or think about how he learned to kiss like that. Cardan Malone is unlike any man I've ever been with before, He does everything differently. I feel a rush of pure adrenaline here and now, just by kissing him. This is not what I was looking for, but my being welcomes him completely.

Cardan kisses me in the same way he does everything else, at a safe pace, without haste, but without giving me a chance to escape.

What does escape my lips are little moans as his tongue sweeps over mine. My hands clench into his sweatshirt, making the space between us disappear.

He kisses me deeper, the hand on my neck tangling at the roots of my hair like he never wants to let me go.

I'm so fucked up and this is just the beginning.

I squirm, panting. His big hard cock is caught between us. It makes my heart race and the emptiness inside me grow bigger. His hands go down my back, grabbing my ass. Lifting me up.

My legs wrap around his slim waist, and he grips me tighter like he's trying to keep me still, but my hips have their own ideas. He is torturing me because he knows what I need, and he is taking his time to deliver it.

He rips his mouth off mine, blinks a few times as if he's trying to focus. The light of a small moment of lucidity flashes in my mind. I should run out of here. Don't let this run its course because I'm sure I'm going to end up smashed into a brick wall. He is dangerous and has a power over me that I had not calculated.

If this is how I feel after a few kisses, what will come after sex?

Cardan is watching me closely, his eyes roaming my face. What is he looking for?

"What are you waiting for?" I ask him.

"For you to regret this," he replies, damn it, perceptive man.

Yes, I want to run away. But not for the reasons that he imagines. It's not because I don't feel, it's because I feel too much.

He ignites a fire in me.

"Let's go to bed," I murmur, my tongue running over my lips. I hope he follows the trail left behind and kisses me until I'm completely disoriented.

This is what I love most about it; with him, I can forget everything.

In an instant, he takes off my cardigan and pulls my shirt over my head. My chest is exposed beneath the thin fabric of my everyday bralette, nothing special but enough to fill a B cup—though you wouldn't know that by the way his eyes darken as his mouth meets my skin.

My nipples harden beneath the material, and my head falls back as I take pleasure in his tongue, his bites. His beard scouring against my delicate skin.

Strands of his thick hair drift between my fingers as I become increasingly desperate for him to make use of his skills.

Yes, we need to get this to a bed, and I hope there is one nearby. Or a sofa, for my purposes it does the same thing.

As if reading my thoughts, Cardan turns away from the door and begins to walk with me wrapped around him. After a few seconds, my back touches something soft and padded.

Yes, finally. A bed.

One by one, he takes off my shoes, then begins to tug at the fabric of my black leggings.

"Are you going to let me see all of you?" he asks, but his eyes don't leave mine.

What does he want from me? Having my body exposed to him in more ways than one.

News flash. He's doing a perfect job all on his own.

I'm lying in front of him wearing only little white cotton panties. I know it won't take long for them to disappear.

The palm of his hand is warm when he rests it on my abdomen, his finger tracing lazy circles on my skin. I close my eyes and focus just on that feeling alone as the fabric runs down my thighs, and then his hand presses down on my legs, opening them for him.

Finally. I want to scream.

And send Pia a thank you message for the wonders of waxing.

The heat from his body sears into me as if gasoline had been thrown onto the fire under my skin. I plead for him to hurry, understanding that he feels the same way.

"Damn it," he answers, settling between my legs with his hard cock pressing against me. His mouth meets mine, and I know no one can provide this pleasure like him.

Though I'm naked, Cardan is still dressed. He wears a snug sweatshirt and shorts, which does little to hide the bulge in them. I gasp and roll my hips against him, begging for relief but never getting enough.

"Why are you dragging this out?" I ask, my eyes still closed.

"Because I don't want to rush you," he says softly, his arms wrapping around me, keeping me captive against him. "I want to ruin you."

That purr escapes my lips, desperate for more of him.

"We're going to do this my way," he continues, those words sounding like both a challenge and a warning. "You have to remember three Malone rules."

My mouth opens to protest, but the only sound that comes out is a groan as he moves my hand over the junction of my legs. The man is an artist.

My lips part to speak, but all that escapes is a moan as his hand slides against the sensitive area between my legs. He's an artist, and I'm almost overcome with pleasure; my hips bucking for more of his touch. No one has ever made me feel like this before.

"My way," he reiterates, his fingers going in and out. Touching me there in the right place. "Three rules... First, there is a strict no clothes policy in my bed."

"This is not your bed," I refute, earning me the removal of his fingers. My body screams in protest.

"If we're in it, it's my bed," he snaps. "Second, ladies first, always."

"Is there number three?"

"You're going to close that little mouth, and you're going to let me do…"

That is not so difficult.

I can't help but think Cardan Malone was born to ruin me, but I don't have time to consider it now. His eyes are fixed on mine as his hand continues its work.

"Trust me, *Bonita*," he says quietly. "I'm going to make you feel so good…"

To prove that what he just said is true the pressure builds up in my core.

I yell his name again, arching my back, my pelvis rocking for more. Making his fingers slide inside me more easily.

A growl reverberates in his chest and echoes off the walls of the room, the need choking me; my mind can't focus on anything other than him and the spell he weaves over me.

Cardan kisses the skin just below my belly button as his finger continues to move in and out of me, slowly. A sound comes out of my throat, my body tenses, I'm looking for relief, and he refuses to give it to me.

"Fuck me, Cardan. Fuck me hard." There it is, I'm asking for what I want.

"No," he says. I want to protest, but his tongue traces my folds, and I start to forget my name. "It's your game, but you will have to play by my rules."

Damn man. I really want to yell at him to fuck off, but he makes fighting hard.

"And one of them is for you to call out my name when you come." To emphasize his statement, his fingers dig into my thighs as he continues to delight in between them.

Without a doubt, he is the one in control when we are in bed, though I have never felt so powerful before. All of my self-doubts and insecurities vanish as Cardan admires my body like it were some masterpiece. This confidence gives me the strength to ask for what I desire—where and how I want it. Every beat of my heart takes me up to a higher level with no plummeting down afterward. The covering on the bed is soft and fluffy, almost forming a cloud beneath me as he lifts me up and keeps me afloat. Afterward, I know I'll need to build my walls back up to protect me, but right now all I want is for him to keep using his magic on me. As his mouth works its sorcery over me, his fingers open me up further. Then his tongue traces circles…

Finally…

"Cardan," letter by letter. Beat by beat. His name is on my lips.

My fingers grab his hair, looking for more friction, more of him.

Wanting it all.

"Are you going to take your clothes off now?" I say in a hopeful voice, my eyes barely open.

He stands up, leaning on his arms, my thighs the perfect frame for his chest.

Made just for me.

"We aren't going to fuck now," he states, and hearing those words, I feel like I've been hit with a bucket of cold water.

I gape at him, now, for a very different reason.

"What?"

"I'm not going to fuck you now. I changed my mind." He seems to refuse to do so, but the package in his shorts tells a very different story. This means I have the potential to change his mind.

"You are the worst fuck-buddy of all, what the fuck are you talking about?"

I have rebuked him, yes, but my legs go around his waist, trying to get him closer to me.

The task is not easy. The man is strong. And right now he is a rock that refuses to move.

"I have my pride, you know?" he says, making me gasp. He has to be kidding me. "What? Do you think you can use me for your orgasms and then forget about me?"

A kiss falls on the tip of my hardened nipple, followed by a small bite. What kind of macabre game is this?

"I'm making sure you come back for more."

My hands flutter down the nape of his neck, over the hard muscles of his shoulders, caressing the tattoo there.

And his mouth… his mouth…

"We have a deal," I insist because the ache between my legs is undeniable.

"I understand," he replies before attacking my other nipple. "But that doesn't mean we can't have a little fun."

"If what you consider fun is to leave me frustrated…"

I want to continue this discussion, tell him to go to hell, but his lips meet mine, and he kisses every one of my complaints away.

Yes, playing is fun, but before you start, you have to consider your opponent.

And never, never underestimate them.

CHAPTER THIRTEEN

The bed is comfortable and warm. The most luxurious I have ever slept in. And I can't stay.

The reason why I can't is because I want to. God, how much I want to stay.

This game is getting dangerous. Playing with fire is dangerous. The alarms in my head are ringing. *Danger. Danger. Runaway while you can, Elena.*

I blink my eyes again. I know this is the first time, but it feels so different.

Crap.

I am twenty-six years old. Twenty fucking six. Why the fuck do I feel like a teenager?

Run for your life, Elena.

Why is this happening so fast?

Moving offers me the first clue.

I'm sore in all the right places; trying to get out of bed takes longer than I thought, mainly because I have to unwind from Cardan's body.

He's so big and takes up so much space. No, it's not that. He has me wrapped like a cocoon of warmth. Holding me tight against his skin, like he wants me to become part of him and never let me go.

What I would give to lift the white sheet that covers it, the temptation is great. So is my fear.

Yes, fear. Fear of not being able to resist him. Fear because he makes me feel everything, too.

Every time those piercing green eyes looked at me last night as he moved inside of me. Making me feel things I shouldn't.

It would be so easy to fall. And so dangerous.

That is why I have to go. This adventure was good and fun. No one has ever done something like this for me, organizing a wonderful weekend in cahoots with my best friend. Never.

Cardan's bet is simple. His target is to make me fall, but everything I want is to fly. I want to open my wings and let the wind take me away. At least while I still can.

Get out of here now, Elena.

The alarm in my head rings again as Cardan moves in bed, hugging me even closer. He seems content to feel me close.

Nothing enters through the windows except the lights on outside. It must be late. Or very early.

The energy this man has, it kept me awake for hours. The fucking, the talking, ordering room service, then repeat.

I search for my clothes scattered on the floor, not without hitting my little finger with the leg of the bed. My right hand flies to my mouth, and I scream and cry silently. Fuck that hurt. But nothing would compare to what is to come if I decide to stay.

Tiptoeing, I get dressed, grab my handbag, and walk out of the room barefoot. Closing the door behind me, making it impossible for me to go back to the hot naked man sleeping on the bed.

Luckily, I don't meet anyone on my walk of shame back to my own room—yes, it's technically his, he paid for it, but what difference does it make.

Destinee is asleep on her stomach in one of the beds, snoring softly. The couple of empty wine bottles that rest on the nightstand give me a clue that the party here was good. Or at least the hangover will be that awaits her.

I will happily supply the chilaquiles, very spicy.

Coming here wasn't enough; there needs to be a land in between. Acres, preferably. My orchard is ideal for that. It's private property. I can call the police.

Coward, screams a voice within me. Yes, *soy una gallina,* a big chicken. They can say here she ran, here she died.

I turn on the lamp on the side of the bed. Dee doesn't even move. Well, that gives me time to pack our things as fast as I can. No, there is no time for a shower, I will do it in the privacy of my room. Yes, as in my house. Where my father has a rifle and knows how to use it.

I'm the apple of his eye. He will be there to defend me.

"Destinee," I call out, shaking her arm. She is dead to the world. "Dee, you have to wake up. We're leaving."

Nothing, my friend just turns her head the other way and continues in Morpheus' arms.

"Destinee, there's a shoe sale at the mall." A smart attempt that pays off immediately. I know my friend well.

She gets out of bed, remaining seated.

"What?" she asks while clutching her head.

"Get up. We're leaving," I tell her, earning one of those looks that tells me that I've grown another head like I've gone completely crazy or something.

"What the fuck did you drink? What happened? We're fine here," she protests, trying to go back to bed, but I won't let her.

We need leave, the sooner the better.

"Why aren't you in the other room?" she asks. "You should be with Cardan, doing a full maintenance check on that engine. Don't tell me that his…"

No, that's not the problem. Everything works for him, his lift pole has no problem, and he knows how to use the tools that God gave him.

"Dee, we really need to get out of here," I implore. This has to work; she's my best friend. She must be on my side, right?

"I don't understand why," she excuses herself. "We came to have fun. You have said for weeks that you want to live an adventure and remove the cobwebs from some parts that we will not mention now. Why, when you finally get what you were looking for, do you want to run away? "

That's the million-dollar question, ladies and gentlemen.

Because even though my heart is broken, I'm not immune. Because my walls won't stop it.

Because I can't resist him.

Although the bible says it, I also remember my grandmother saying it, to flee from temptation. Sacred word it is. Not even my smart-ass friend can argue with that.

"Can we go?" I ask her as I flop onto the bed in front of her. "Dee, this isn't what I thought it would be. Cardan…"

She studies me for a couple of minutes in silence.

"Don't tell me Cardan is one of those guys who likes to tie women and make them pay for being mischievous. I can handle it. But if we are talking about needles, excrement… no, I agree. Dealing with them at the hospital is ok, but mixed with sex is a big no. We have to get out of here."

Her nonsense makes me smile, although my smile is sad.

"It's not that," I explain and realizing I'm doing also for myself. "But I feel like I was ambushed, Dee."

There's no other way to put it. She waves her hand for me to continue speaking.

"He's not playing fair. He's looking for more than I can give him."

Destinee moves, taking my shaking hands in hers.

"And that's a bad thing because…"

I get up suddenly and carelessly. "Because he deceived me," I squeal in panic. My breathing is shallow and agitated. "So get up and get dressed, we're getting out of here. I got the keys to your car, so don't doubt that I won't leave you here."

Destinee gives me a killer look but doesn't say another word.

The journey back home, while the sun peeks over the horizon, seems very long.

♡♡♡

"What are you doing here?" A male voice asks me when I find myself in the kitchen of the house.

"I live here," I reply without moving from where I am. Standing in front of the sink, where I just put down the glass of water I had.

Destinee and I arrived at home about ten minutes ago, she made a beeline to my room, and I came to the kitchen looking for something to do.

And it looks like I'm actually going to have a lot to do.

We have company.

"Smartass," he tells me.

"Idiot," I accuse him. "Did you forget your manners in San Francisco or what?"

He immediately comes over to hug me.

"Squirt," he says as he squeezes me. "Dad said we weren't expecting you until later. What happened, Destinee and you decided you didn't need the tune-up?"

Ugh, if he only knew what kind of tune-up we're talking about…

We both laugh, although I do it for a completely different reason.

My brother, Ruben, leans away to look at me, and from the sparkle in his eyes I can imagine what is to come.

"Elena is home," he yells, unleashing pandemonium. And to emphasize those words, there is thunder outside.

No, I didn't mean figuratively. A storm is coming.

I can kiss the relaxing Sunday I had planned goodbye. The last thing I'm going to have is peace with my four brothers at home, but on second thought, it is the perfect distraction.

Just what I need to keep my mind occupied to stop thinking about my maintenance provider...

"Are we going to have breakfast or what?" David yells after kissing me on the cheek.

That, of course, means are you going to make breakfast for us?

Luckily the pantry is well stocked, and we have a few things ready to warm up in the fridge.

Sopes de machaca with refried beans to start. In the freezer, I'm sure, there is pozole I could reheat. Which by the way, tastes much better that way. My brothers have bottomless pits for stomachs, so I'm sure they'll be hungry again in a couple of hours. My father better have charcoal because *carne asada* tacos are the best option to feed them all. *Salsa verde* made with roasted chiles is my specialty.

The next two hours are spent in a whirlwind of activity, frying the *sopes*, and mashing the *refrito* beans... authentic Mexican food is delicious but hard to make.

Also, my older brother, Gabriel, has brought his girlfriend Erin, a girl with long blonde hair and an easy smile. They have been together for a couple of years now; my father likes her very much, and she was extremely helpful when things got crazy around here after my mother passed away. We all consider her part of the family. I hope my brother decides to make it official soon, I could use a sister, and my father will have some reason to celebrate. It may be pouring outside, but it's warm here. My family is together again.

Destinee appears at the kitchen door as we sit down, she just took a shower, so she looks half decent.

Suddenly, David seems to take a particular interest in spreading beans in his sope, while Destinee greets everyone and sips horchata like her life depends on it. My father doesn't know what to do. Ruben is looking at them conspiratorially, as if he is ready to make a few jokes at David and Destinee's expense, I think they have held back because I have a knife in my hand and I'm not very subtle about it. What an uncomfortable situation, if my brother hadn't been such an idiot...

But that's a story for another day, and it's not mine to tell anyway.

And why suddenly does Martin look like he's ready to get the hell outta here?

"Lena, Dad told me you're making headway in the mango business..." I give Gabriel a grateful look, who has started a safe topic. "Do you have some samples we could try?"

None of my brothers need time to accept fruits with chili, dehydrated or not, they love it.

"I need to take some of this home," Erin squeaks, still with her mouth full. "This is great, Lena."

"The secret is in the chili, babe," my brother replies, moving his eyebrows. Eww... he seems to have forgotten that we are all around the table, and the last thing I want to know is what my brother does with his... chili.

All jokes aside, I turn to see my father, who smiles as he leans back in his chair. He has a smile on his lips while his eyes are full of joy but also nostalgia. It is the first time everyone has come home since those difficult days. It is so good to be together.

"If you need any help, you know we're here for you," Martin tells me, taking my hand in his. "If you need funding, just tell me. Whatever."

That's so nice of him to say. Martin had always been a very quiet, nerdy kind of guy, thick, black-rimmed glasses and all. Always going out to fish and solving complicated math equations. I always wondered if he would turn out to be some kind of professor, but now he's a tech mogul and lives in the San Francisco area, making tons of money. I hope that makes his heart feel full. My brother is a good guy and deserves all the happiness in the world.

"I think everything here is under control; for now, the production is quite small. I want to start with a stand down the farmers' market and at the general store, we will see in a few months where the wind takes us."

"We all started somewhere, Lena," this time, it's Ruben speaking; the party guy is gone, and the loving brother is here. "Let me know if you need help to create an LLC. I'll take care of anything you need. We are proud of you for doing more than just following the family tradition. You're writing your own story."

A knot of tears threatens to choke me.

"There is nothing wrong with following the family tradition, running the orchard isn't easy," my father intervenes. He knows what it means to work here, and so do my brothers. We all grew up the same way.

"No one denies it," Gabriel says as he holds up his hands in surrender. "But Lena is starting a new business, out of her comfort zone. And for that, we should all be proud."

"Salud!," says my father raising his glass of horchata. "For Lena and her new business!"

Voices echo, my brothers, Erin and Destinee, say out loud as well.

When the shouting ceases, we hear a knock on the door.

"I'll go," Martin shouts while walking away.

'And since we don't call each other here without shouting, my brother does it again, this time from the foyer.

"Elena Maria, come here. You have a special delivery." There is an unmistakable hint of humor in his voice.

Destinee looks at me like she planned it. After what happened, it would not surprise me one bit.

I walk to the foyer, not sure of what I am going to find there.

But my knees are shaking, while I realize it's not an actual package.

"What are you doing here?" I tell him when I realize that he's there, standing on the porch of my house, with his jacket and hair soaked.

"Did you think you were going to get rid of me that easily?" Cardan asks, putting his hands to his chest. "You left me all heartbroken, Elena."

That makes me smile, even though I have to bite my lip, so he doesn't realize I'm doing it. And I roll my eyes for dramatic effect.

"You didn't answer. What are you doing here?"

"Who is this?" my brother asks, not Martin who answered the door, but a different one. Because obviously, they are all about the tea, of course, my other three brothers are behind me witnessing everything, without missing a single detail.

Dammit.

CHAPTER FOURTEEN

"Cardan!" Destinee screams behind me.

"Cardan," my father greets him as he extends his hand.

"Cardan?" my brothers ask at the same time, identical frowns painted on their faces.

"Welcome," my father tells him. "These are my sons. We're all eating in the kitchen. Do you want to join us?"

Ah, my father is a gentleman. Always. But why is he inviting Cardan to eat with us today?

Oh, I know. Dad is waiting for one of my brothers to do his dirty work. Or have all of them work as a team. Some to torture him, another to dismember him, and the other is in charge of making the evidence disappear?

"Who's this *gabacho?*" David asks, inspecting Cardan head to toe.

"Shut up, *cholo!*" I tell him. There's nothing that my brothers hate more than people giving them nicknames because we are Latino. Beaners, wet-backs, we've heard them all. Although, we're all here legally, I mean, we were born and bred in Sunny Hills, for Pete's sake. But there is always an asshole who thinks themselves better than us just for our ancestry or skin color.

My brothers keep throwing out questions randomly, Erin wants to know what's going on, and even Destinee has something to say. Yes, our home has become a madhouse.

"Are they going to let him in the house or are they going to wait for him to get pneumonia?" my father yells, ending this nonsense. "David, get him a towel."

Of course, my brother does what my father asks of him—cross that out—what he was ordered. Spitting out a few words in Spanish, I prefer not to repeat any of them.

Following my father's orders, much to my brothers' dismay, Cardan leaves his boots and jacket in the mudroom and joins us in the kitchen a few minutes later.

Destinee hasn't stopped smiling like the Cheshire cat. Anyone could swear that he came to see her.

"Don't tell me you're not happy to see him," she tells me, moving her eyebrows suggestively.

Erin walks over to us, glaring at me with little stars twinkling in her gray eyes. "He's so dreamy, Lena. Showing up like this in the middle of this downpour. With your brothers here and your father…"

Oh God, I'm already getting hives. What happened to family solidarity? Trenches were supposed to be built, weapons out—everything except allowing Cardan Malone to get close to me.

"I hope you like pozole," my father tells Cardan as he serves him the soup in a rather deep bowl.

"Gringo," shouts Ruben. "I hope you're not one to put cheddar cheese on your tacos. Or lettuce."

The other three assholes laugh, and my father makes a sound that's like a growl.

"Stop the bullying," I yell, my voice coming out of nowhere. It's enough. "You guys are idiots."

"Let's eat," my father snaps. My brothers are all in their thirties, but they follow orders when they hear his authoritative tone.

"I must say," Destinee says, leaning on me a bit. "These aren't the green chilaquiles I was promised, but you know I can't resist pozole. Your mother's recipe is the best."

"It's the only one you've tried," I teasingly say while jokingly pushing her away.

But what my friend says is true, there's nothing like the food my mother used to make.

"This is delicious," says Cardan, wiping his mouth with a cloth napkin. "Thank you for having me."

I can't help it; seeing him here with my family makes me smile. Broadly.

Until my brother David opens his mouth to say, "Not willingly."

"David Alejandro!" my father, Destinee, and I yell in unison.

"I can't believe I've raised assholes," Dad complains, looking at Cardan apologizingly. But he's fresh as a cucumber, eating the soup my mother taught me how to make. He's a worldly man. He's used to managing crises and commanding a large group of mechanics... my brothers are not a challenge.

"What about you, Cardan, do you have any siblings?" Erin asks, breaking the silence.

Cardan smiles and tells her about his family. His mother, of course. He doesn't say anything about his father; that's a delicate matter for him.

After we finish eating, my brothers clean the kitchen while Erin and Destinee bake blueberry white chocolate chunk cookies. With the pack of wild boars contained, I take the opportunity to speak with Cardan in the privacy of my office.

"What are you doing here?" I ask him as soon as I close the door behind me.

He looks at me silently for one heartbeat and then another. Then a smile pulls his lips up. "Did you think I wasn't going to come after you?"

Cardan takes two sure steps forward, effectively trapping me between his body and the door.

Why are his movements so calculated? And why the hell can't I think when he is near me?

What is happening to me?

It must be those green eyes. Or the beard. Could it be his arms? Or his cologne?

Less than two minutes alone, and I'm already overwhelmed.

That's the problem. He fills every inch of space, leaving no room for anything else.

He becomes the air I need to breathe.

Everything is him.

"Did you think it was going to end after our night together?"

This man is as stubborn as a mule, and he refuses to accept what I've told him. My words were very clear. An adventure, that's all I'm looking for; that's all I have to give.

And the adventure didn't include him showing up at my house and having dinner with my family. Especially with my brothers here.

"This wasn't the deal, Cardan," I scold him.

"Deals can always be renegotiated."

"Not ours," I say assured. "This is what it is; take it or leave it."

There's no more. I told him in Napa, and I'm just repeating it now.

"What? So all you want is for me to do things to you in the dark but never see you in the light?"

Fuck, why is it so hard to make him understand? Why can't he follow my rules?

Isn't it any man's dream to fuck without strings attached?

Why did I find the only one of the species who chose not to take advantage of that?

"What do you want, Cardan?"

"Making you mine." Those words hit me right in the chest. They're like a wrecking ball.

"That's not possible," I yell at him when I catch my breath.

"So what? I can shove it up your ass, but can't I stay and spend the night?"

I wish I could say that he is finally understanding, but the anger is palpable in his tone of voice. His face is flushed. My heart is pounding in my chest. I can hear it drumming in my ears.

Three quick knocks are heard, and no, Cardan didn't take out his anger on the walls. The door opens, and my brother pops his head in.

"What now, Gabriel?" I ask him, still looking at Cardan.

"We heard your screams all over the house…"

"Don't worry, man," Cardan replies. "I'm leaving."

And he goes without saying another word.

I stay in the same place, under my brother's scrutinizing gaze. Part of me wants to go after him and yell at him that we haven't finished our discussion. The other wants to throw myself at his feet and beg him to stay.

With him, I feel everything.

And that's the problem.

The house seems to have gone silent, while in the distance we hear a car door slam shut, and the roar of an engine driving away.

Now, I don't have to deal with him anymore. Only the feelings he left me behind with.

I walk away from the wall and try to compose myself.

"What are you doing?" Gabriel asks me.

"Preparing to face the music." Which means the looks and sarcasm from my brothers and probably a conversation with my father.

"No, Lena," he cuts me off. "What are you doing with your life in general? That's the reason we came because we are worried about you. *Papá* told us that you refused to see Dax, but you didn't want to hear a word about him. Then that man shows up here and we all hoped it was a sign that you've decided to face the future. With the challenges and everything that it means. We think that maybe that would be a good reason to fight."

"Us? You all came together to conspire against me?"

He looks at me before answering.

"*Papá* too, but don't be mad. It's his job to make sure the apple of his eye is thriving."

I take a deep breath, not knowing what to say.

Unsure of whether there is a death sentence over my head.

"None of you know what it's like to be in my shoes. You all have all your life to live and a chance to be happy." I think for a moment about my mother's life, and her death before answering. "Sometimes I think it would have been better not to know about this, look at mom. She lived her life without the pressure of knowing."

A thick tear rolls down my cheek. Gabriel's eyes begin to water.

"The coin always has two sides, Lena," he mutters. "Ignorance is bliss, yes. But haven't you thought that if she had the opportunity to undergo treatment, she would still be here with us?"

We would all give anything to have her here. I know that I miss her beyond words. If she were here, everything would be different.

But it's not as painful to think about what is. Although her absence hurts me, I must learn to live with my reality.

"I know you've been looking for adventure, *hermanita*. If that's what you want to do, live your life to the fullest, and take responsibility for enjoying every day within your reach. None of us know which day will be our last."

What Gabriel says is true. But I'm scared to death.

"Do you remember what Mom said? God sometimes breaks our hearts to show us what we are capable of."

My heart is broken in more ways than one.

"I don't know what to do, Gab."

My brother looks at me and smiles tenderly, for a moment, I see my father reflected in his eyes.

"The first thing we're going to do is get you out of here so you can go talk to Cardan..."

"But... but... I want to stay here with you guys."

"I promise you that we'll see each other again very soon."

Raising his hand, waiting for me to take it. After a couple of seconds, I do, and my brother leads me out to the side door.

"Be happy, Lena," he says before giving me a kiss on the cheek and a pat on the back. "It's what we all want for you."

I think I'm ready for us to be awesome together.

CHAPTER FIFTEEN

I'm standing outside Cardan's apartment door, feeling more nervous than ever.

What am I going to do if he rejects me?

This is worse than the day at Free Fall. Now I'm jumping without a parachute.

I knock on the door and wait for an answer.

A couple of minutes pass, and nothing. I repeat the action, this time with my fist. Strong and with purpose. I know he's here, his car is parked, at least the two I've seen. With this rain, I don't think anyone in their right mind would venture outside the house.

"What?" he says as he opens the door, his hair is wet, and he's wearing only a towel around his narrow hips.

"I came to see you." Duh, of course something so clever had to come out of my mouth.

Cardan looks at me for a moment. Not a word leaves his mouth, but I can see his nipples getting hard. I want to bite them and run my hands over his bare chest and lose myself in him. My fingers itch to stroke his beard. His hair.

"What do you want, Elena?"

"To be yours," I tell him before throwing myself into his arms without giving him a chance to answer me.

At first, he stands still. The optimistic part of me believes that it is just from the surprise. After that, his lips part to receive mine, and his strong arms hold me against his body.

Suddenly, he pulls back so that his hands can hold my face steady as he stares into my eyes.

"Are you sure? No more boundaries between the two of us."

No, I'm not sure, but I'm getting closer to the cliff.

"Catch me when I fall," I murmur.

"Can't you see it?" His expression turns serious. Sincerity shines brightly in those green eyes. "I'm there falling with you."

The air is gone. It's getting harder and harder for me to breathe. My heart is beating hard; for the first time, I'm ready to embrace this feeling.

I want to give Cardan the key that opens the cage allowing us to fly. To fly high. But my wings are broken, and not even he, with all his tools, can fix them.

His hands move down toward my waist, then rests above my butt, pulling my body against his. My nipples needing attention in the confines of my bra.

It's raining outside, but a fire has ignited in here between us. And he's pouring gasoline on the flames.

Cardan bows his head. His beard, tickling my cheeks, my neck. Baby Jesus, this is torture.

Luckily, everything speeds up. Feeling his naked body over my dressed one makes me feel powerful. And at the same time, I'm at his mercy.

He backs me into the wall while closing the door with his heel. Cardan doesn't waste time tearing all the clothing off my body. Thank God for my leggings; they are so easy to remove. Our hands move fast, seeking naked flesh, our lips peppering kisses.

Five minutes after arriving at his door, he's fucking me silly. Driving his hard cock into my warm, welcoming body again, again, and again. It feels almost like he's punishing me for refusing him before.

Stop this torture, Cardan. Give me more...

I wrap my legs around his hard body and claw at his shoulders with my fingers, clinging for dear life. I need him close; every time he thrusts inside me, I feel he's making a statement. Yes, he wants me to know who I belong to. Whispering his name in the darkness of the room, just for him to listen, like a prayer as the orgasm runs through my body like an avalanche, so intense.

My broken heart is bursting; it's so full.

I can't breathe. I can't think.

I just want to feel free in his arms.

We look at each other, smiling. This is happening.

"This is real," I whisper.

In the shadows, I can see his eyes glitter, full of emotions. This is what you feel when you're falling.

It's terrifying, exhilarating.

"You're here, *bonita*," he says, pointing to his heart. My face in his hands, our breaths mingling. "And I won't let you go."

"I'm not going anywhere. I don't want to."

CHAPTER SIXTEEN

Time flies when there's something fun occupying your thoughts.

I spend my days in the orchard with my father, supervising the planting of the new trees and the tiling with compost of the old ones. I have also started to sell my dried fruit in a couple of shops in town, Cardan made a big order, and now, at the garage countertops, there is a stand with my products for his guests to enjoy while waiting for their cars. The marketing is working wonders. I'm getting direct orders and had to call Martin for help to set up a new webpage. My next stop is to visit other small shops as soon as the mango harvest begins in the summer. Right now at the top of my production capacity.

Now let me tell you about my nights… My nights pass between the soft sheets of Cardan's bed.

He's also been swamped. We aren't the honeyed couple who are hung up on each other all the time. Cardan has received two classic cars for restoration, and getting the parts is not an easy task. He has been traveling across the country to auctions to get them. The animosity has calmed down a bit with other mechanics in town as they have stopped seeing him as public enemy number one.

There is enough business for everyone, gentlemen.

"When are you going to see Dax?" my father asks me. That is the same question I keep hearing for weeks now. The answer remains the same.

"I don't know. Some day when I'm sure of what I want."

My father purses his lips into a thin line. I'm sure it's so he doesn't start an argument.

We have talked about this many times without getting anywhere.

"Time is golden, girl. If your mother…"

My heart sinks. He is not playing fair. He knows that playing the mom card is powerful.

"Now, I have other things to worry about." And that's true, I look at my dehydrator in front of me. The damn thing refuses to work.

"Why don't you call the manufacturer?" my father says, and I want to roll my eyes.

The thing is, to save a few pennies, I bought the device secondhand. So I have no one to complain to.

As they say, cheap is expensive. I should definitely invest in a good dehydrator and buy the extended warranty.

"Do you know anyone in town who knows how to fix these things?"

"Maybe Tom," he replies, referring to the man who fixes refrigerators and stuff.

It's not a bad idea. I'm considering it when we hear a loud knock on the door.

My father looks at the watch on his wrist. t's shortly before noon. "I'll go see who it is," he announces before leaving. A couple of minutes later, he returns to the kitchen Cardan in tow.

"Hey," I greet him, as by the corner of my eye, I see him taking a look at what I'm wearing – leggings, as usual, and one of my sweatshirts with the orchard's logo. Internally I shrug, if he doesn't like it, he should have called first. He looks as delicious as ever. Those worn jeans he wears to work fit him like a glove. "I didn't expect to see you so early."

Cardan smiles, and although his smile touches his eyes, there is something more to it.

This man has plans, and they aren't the type that I like so much. There is something else.

"I have something for you," he announces after kissing me on the cheek. The short hairs on his beard make me itch. My body churns for more. But we are in the kitchen, and my father is with us.

"Which means this isn't a social visit," I state.

"More like a bribe. Are you coming?" He ends his words by pointing to the door.

Curiosity is a powerful weapon; I go to the entrance of the house, walking fast. When I get there, I find several cardboard boxes stacked on top of each other.

"They're peaches," he murmurs in my ear. "I couldn't help but remember you in those pants that aren't pants."

To emphasize what was said, he slaps me on the ass, making me jump.

"No need to get politically correct, Malone," I chide him. "Thanks for the peaches, but I can't do anything with them; the dehydrator is broken. And don't bruise the merchandise unless you're going to buy it."

Cardan puts his hands on my waist, pulling my body against his. These pants are comfortable, but they are so thin that I can feel everything. His... his eggplant... yes, pun intended.

"That has an easy solution, baby. Let's go to my home."

"And the peaches?" I quickly count the boxes, eighteen.

"Your peach is going to be very good when we finish. I can assure you." Mmmm... this has potential. Wearing these pants, I can feel his body turning harder as he hugs me closer.

I elbow him in the ribs, although my lady parts beg me to accept his proposal.

"I have work to do this afternoon. Also, the dehydrator thing. My father knows someone in Sunny Hills who may be able to help."

"Do you have any tools?" he asks me. "I can take a look."

That makes me smile as I move in his arms and face him.

"Wow, Malone, you do have hidden talents."

He raises his eyebrows suggestively before answering. "Never underestimate the power of a man who knows how to use his tools."

Oh, boy. *Forget the dehydrator; take me home, Malone. Show me how good you are with that hammer.*

Sadly, there are urgent matters pressing for my attention. "How many more of those phrases do you have up your sleeve?"

"Two or three," he replies before giving me one last butt squeeze. "Let's get this over with. The faster we finish, the faster I can have you for myself."

Twenty minutes later, Cardan has my dehydrator fan disassembled on the kitchen table. While he's busy checking the appliance, I'm washing the peaches and placing them in plastic crates lined with paper towels. Hopefully, Cardan can fix it, so tonight, I'll start dehydrating the fruit. I'll be lucky if I have enough chili for all this.

"The wiring around the fan is rusted," he tells me after a while. We both have been working while music by The Flaming Lips is playing from the speaker. "One of the guys from the garage is going to bring me something so that we can put it in to get this to operate properly. Now let's talk about payment for my services."

I turn around to look at him. A few steps separate us, but we are alone in the kitchen. Cardan is sitting near the table, and I am still standing in front of the sink.

"Yes, I remember now. This peach thing was nothing more than blackmail."

"A bribe," he clarifies, smirking. "Which is very different."

"A bribe," I repeat. "May I know what for?"

There is that smile again. *Panties, stay in place. My father is somewhere in the house, and we have work to do.*

"Chief Malone came to the shop this morning," he explains. "He invited us to have dinner with his family on Saturday."

I look at him with my mouth open. Cardan agreed to go to the Malone house just like that?

"What happened? Why the change of heart?"

He rises from the chair, closing the distance between us. "Because I was talking to my mother. And we both want answers. I'm the new kid on the block, but it seems like here there is a story ready to be unveiled."

"Do you think you are related?" Cardan doesn't talk much about his family. He has only told me a few things about his mother and his stepfather Dick, who he sees as his father.

"My mother doesn't know much either, so I'm looking for some answers. It will be a good place to start."

Well, this is a change of heart. Cardan is opening up. Not just with me, but the whole world.

"You know that Griffin will be there, right?"

"Since it is his parents' house, I was expecting it," he says looking into my eyes. "That is why I'm going to bring reinforcements. You'll be there to guard me."

That makes me laugh out loud.

Cardan doesn't need anyone to guard him. But I understand the need for moral support.

Stepping into unfamiliar territory is never easy. And, after all, it's about his possible family.

"You didn't need to bring me a dozen and a half boxes of peaches to bribe me. With some attention to my peach, I would have said yes."

"Now it turns out that I'm more than just a pretty face," he whispers as his arms go around my waist.

"Sure, there is no way I could forget about your ability to handle tools."

"And the fact that I have a lift pole at your complete disposal." Oh yeah, I can feel said pole poking my hip.

"The advantages of having one of those…"

"Ahem…" someone clears his throat. Cardan and I part ways like a couple of teenagers who have been caught.

"Dad," I squeal as Cardan says, "Mr. Posada…"

"Hmm… I ran into one of the guys from the shop who came to bring this," he snaps as he hands Cardan a paper bag.

"Thanks, this is what we needed to finish the dehydrator."

"Sure…" my father mutters under his breath. "You guys were very busy with that…"

I give Cardan the stink eye. We are in my family's home, after all.

"Hurry up," I tell Cardan as my father lazily walks through the kitchen. "Then you have to help me cut all these peaches into pieces. Where did you get so many?"

"A truck arrived at the garage with a broken engine. The poor man was giving away the fruit on the street. I bought everything left from him at market price."

That makes me smile, and something in my chest tightens. Why does he have to be so perfect? Not only is he willing to give me the adventure I was looking for, but he's also sweet, loving, and considerate. So freaking good in the sack.

If only I could stay with him forever.

Stop, Elena, just stop. You won't get anywhere thinking that way. The only thing you have is the present. Live. Because you don't know what will happen tomorrow.

"Who knew, Cardan Malone? It turns out you are a decent guy."

That makes him laugh. "I did tell you that I am more than just a pretty face."

"And you bought yourself a date for dinner on Saturday."

"Alright," he agrees as he begins to connect the cables that go into my dehydrator again. "And pack a bag. We have plans for Sunday morning."

CHAPTER SEVENTEEN

After finishing with a thousand peaches—I'm not exaggerating, there are around sixty peaches in a box of twenty-five pounds. I should be beaten and ready for bed, but my body is energized. I feel invigorated.

Well, I'm ready to go to bed, just not to sleep.

Cardan said a bag for Saturday night would be needed, but he made me pack for tonight, too. This happens almost three times a week, and he frequently tells me I should leave stuff at his place.

Honestly, I don't know what is stopping me. Stubbornness, the little voice in my head murmurs, yeah, a little bit of that. It sounds so serious and *girlfriendish*, and we haven't talked about titles yet.

"I'd like to fuck you as soon as we get home," he says; his green gaze is on the road before us; those words made my center clench. I want that, too. "But after all the work, I must jump in the shower first."

"I don't care," I reply with a shrug. I don't. I love the way he tastes, and I want him now.

"I do," he counters. "We are playing tonight, testing your boundaries." Oh my… call the fire department, tell them to be alert. "I've fantasized with that ass of yours since the moment we met at Free Fall."

His hands grip the steering wheel harder as if he were making an effort to go home without stopping on the road for a quickie to quench his thirst. At least temporarily. Little he knows, I have a surprise tucked in my bag, and knowing him the way I do... *wait, fucking wait.* We definitely sound like a couple. What happened to my plans? When did I change this much?

Where did I lose the fear?

His deep voice stops the train of my thoughts. "But first, I want those pouty lips wrapped around my cock."

My panties are soaking for him. "Cardan," I whisper, turning to him.

"Yeah?"

"Hurry up," saying these words, my hand lands on his lap, gripping his already hard cock. "Hurry up or stop right here."

No one is around. Our farm is on the outskirts of town, so no one would drive around here unless they have to.

His foot is heavy on the speed, and after the longest ten minutes ever, we finally are parking at the garage.

"Make yourself at home," he says, closing the door behind us. "I'll be back in a minute."

While he walks up the stairs to the second floor, I take some time to make a plan. The street lamps dimly light the apartment, and the thick carpet under the coffee table offers the perfect setting. Plus, we haven't fuck in the living room yet, and that issue that needs to be rectified. Now.

A few minutes later, my clothing is folded in a corner, and I'm waiting for him to come and find me.

"*Bonita?*" I freaking love every time he calls me that way.

"I'm here."

My heart is beating in sync with every step he takes; he's gloriously naked, drying his hair with a towel, but the movement stops as soon as his gaze finds me. The distance between us evaporates.

"Seems like my *bonita* made plans on her own." His hand is on my chin, lifting it so our eyes meet. In the shadows, his green irises are glistening, hypnotizing me. "A man could be used to this."

My heart thuds in my chest as I kneel at his feet in a submissive stance. I'm not a sub per se, but he said something about playing tonight, right?

"You look so beautiful, my love," he whispers, and my heart skips a beat. This is the first time he uses the four-letter word. "But you will look even better while you suck my cock."

He doesn't have to ask me twice; I'm already salivating.

My lips come closer to his crown, and I can sense each cell in his body reacting to my proximity. Power surges through me at the thought of having such an effect on him. He looks infinitely large from my vantage point, and I feel like a goddess. I'm in control here. My panties are soaked with anticipation as his hips move in search of more contact with me. But it's not just him who is rushing towards the finish line; my hand instinctively travels to my throbbing center in my quest for release.

"No," he growls, bending down and capturing my arm in one swift movement. "Your orgasms are mine."

He is right; he has coaxed moans out of me. Yes, every time I come, his name is on my lips. Not missing a beat, his foot slips between my legs, and a surge of electricity washes over me as I join him eagerly in this dance we have started.

The fire inside me intensifies as every part of him reacts under my touch—I want nothing more than for this feeling to last forever because I know very well that Cardan Malone means trouble—he has blurred my lines so much that sex is no longer just sex anymore.

One second, I'm kneeling, and the next, he has me on my feet, diving his tongue deep into my mouth, thrusting and lunging until my desire drips down my thigh.

"You're almost there," he murmurs against my lips when I draw back from his lavish kisses. His voice sends another lightning bolt through me as I answer by nodding my head.

"I want you back on your knees. With those gorgeous lips wrapped around my dick."

"Yes, sir." Adrenaline rushes throughout my body as I follow his command. The second my lips curl around him, I suck down, and he groans, thrusting his hips toward me. I swallow deeply at the intensity of his overpowering orgasm. The quakes that course through his entire body make me wish to never let go.

"You are so good at that, my sweet *bonita*." As he carefully wipes the droplet from my lips, his words come out in a silky-smooth purr that washes over me like a warm wave. Cardan always knows just how to make me feel special. I lick the tiny bead of liquid off my lips and flash him a toothy grin.

Suddenly, he scoops me up, tossing me over his shoulder like a grain sack. I can feel his powerful muscles bunching and flexing under my body as he moves me effortlessly across the room. The way his hands grip my flesh sends shivers down my spine.

"Are you ready to play?" He growls throatily, smacking my ass firmly as we move. His voice is like pure sex, making my heart race with anticipation. I nod eagerly, knowing that whatever he has planned for us will be amazing. "Working with all those peaches gave me some ideas."

I'm putty in his hands, desperate for whatever twists and turns he has planned next.

CHAPTER EITHTEEN

The rest of the week flies by. Dee and Cardan's help was very much needed to pack the dried peaches. Taking advantage of my father's contacts, I was able to sell some at two local markets, and the people from the general store called me twice to replenish their stock.

My business is booming, with the past days sales, I'll be able to buy fruit from other orchards and start with new products, but for now, the list will keep short. Peaches, mangoes, and pineapples. Following his advice, my brother Ruben and I discussed the formation of a new company to keep my finances separate from the orchard.

I'm chatting nonstop while Cardan mostly gives me one-word answers and some grunts while driving his Jeep across the town's roads toward west.

"Don't be nervous," I tell him as I put my hand on his knee. We're on our way to Malone's house for dinner. "Griffin and his family are lovely people."

Another grunt to emphasize the words he's about to say. "You mean the bastard who showed up in my office to scare my employees and clients? Yes, he's a good guy."

I tap him on the shoulder before speaking. "We all have our bad moments and shouldn't be judged for them."

Cardan rolls his eyes and stops the car at a red light.

"I'd put that little mouth of yours to good use, but we are almost there." His words give me goosebumps. I love sucking him dry, and my palm is already on his knee. He takes my hand and places it over the bulge hidden under the zipper of his jeans.

Oh, I'd be happy to comply, but he's right. There is no time.

"Remember what they say about anticipation," I remind him, though my fingers itch to play along.

"You are going to pay when…"

"Oh look, that's the Malone's home," I squeal as I point to the house to our left.

"Two can play this game, Elena," he mutters before turning off the Jeep and hurrying out the door to help me out.

As I watch him walk around the front of the vehicle, I think. Bring it. This is a game for two.

But first, we have to get through this dinner.

We walk hand in hand down the driveway to the house. It's my first time here, the Malones are friends with my brothers, but they are all older than me, and we never moved in the same circles. Oh great… now we're both nervous.

We climb the steps that lead to the porch, and before we can knock on the door, it opens. The famous Sheriff Robert Malone welcomes us with a smile. It doesn't matter that he retired years ago; for us here around town, he'll always be the Sheriff. Next to him is a boy with dark hair and blue eyes. If memory serves me right, it's Liam, one of his grandsons.

"Welcome," he greets us. "Nice to see you, Elena. It is good to have you over for dinner."

"Thanks for having us," Cardan replies as he offers his hand.

"Becca," Sheriff Malone yells while we enter his home, a craftsman with beige-painted walls full of family pictures. "Our guests are here…" We notice her short silver hair as she comes to greet us.

"Welcome, it's a pleasure finally to meet you," she offers Cardan her open hand and a broad smile, then turns to look at me. "Oh, how beautiful you look, Elena. I haven't seen you since before Christmas…" She cuts off her words, I know what she means. We haven't seen each other since my mother's funeral.

Cardan hands her the flowers he brought along with a bottle of wine.

"Isn't it lovely?" she says while fixing her eyes on me. "The Malone boys are dangerous, Elena. Once you get your eye on them, no one can resist."

"That's right, woman," her husband chides her. But his eyes are full of love and humor. "Come on, we set the table on the patio, and the boys are already there."

The next minutes are filled with introductions and greetings ass well as Griffin's apologies. Like I told Cardan, he's a good guy. We all have our moments.

Also, Daisy, his daughter, is an adorable little girl. With the same strawberry blonde hair as her mother and dimples that appear on her cheeks every time she smiles. And that is often.

The Malone boys have fallen prey to the charm of the little girl who, at her young age, has everyone—including Liam—eating out of the palm of her hand.

"So," Graham, the younger brother, begins. "Are you from Los Angeles? What made you choose a small town like Sunny Hills to set up your business?"

Very subtle, Graham. Starting with the big guns, I see…

"I thought the detective was the other one…" Cardan mutters under his breath. At the same time, Malory slaps her husband on the arm.

"You came for answers," I whisper back, reminding him of what we discussed.

Cardan breathes before answering, the businessman is talking over. "The truth was it was a matter of luck. I was looking for a small place near a city, with good access roads and tax advantages. I have this business idea that I am starting, and it seemed like a good idea to come here."

It makes me want to take out the fireworks, he answered more than two questions, and without the need of a gun pointed at him. Bravo!

"And your family?" This time it's Gideon, the middle brother, who asks him.

Cardan makes a long, heavy pause before replying. "I only have my father's name on my birth certificate. Since I can remember, it's been my mother and me. Well, she remarried... but you know what I mean."

The Sheriff clears his throat before speaking. "What is your father's name?"

"Mike Malone," he responds like the syllables have a bitter taste.

Everyone falls silent. I think there is a jaw or two touching the floor.

"Mike, you say?" asks the Sheriff once he has regained his composure.

"Correct. And that's all I have. He left my mother and me more than thirty-seven years ago and never looked back." Cardan confirms the news. "And my mother had to break her back working two shifts to support us and also pay the debts the bastard left behind."

The Sheriff shifts in his seat and looks at his wife, who also seems quite uncomfortable. I think coming here wasn't such a good idea after all.

"I'm sure he had good reasons, son," the man finally says.

Cardan looks as if the man just slapped him. "What reasons can justify abandoning his wife with a baby?"

Another silence ensues that seems eternal.

"Death." It's Griffin who says it. "Mike Malone died in late eighty-two."

Cardan is left with his mouth open, not knowing how to reply. The deep lines on his face and the fact his hand flew looking for mine, gives me the answer.

"How do you know?" I dare to ask.

"Because he was my brother," replies the Sheriff with a heavy sigh. "We didn't always agree, nor did we get along as well as expected. But Mickey was my younger brother."

Cardan's face contorts with pain, shock, and sorrow upon hearing the news of his father's passing. My own heart breaks for him as I think of the loving memories I have with my own mother. The pain radiating from him feels like a spear stabbing through my chest, urging me to find a way to give him comfort. Taking his hand in mine, I grasp it tightly, wishing with all my might that there was something more I could do.

"You want a beer?" Giddeon finally asks.

"More like a double whiskey," Cardan replies without looking at him, while rubbing his beard with his free hand. His gaze is lost, I think the poor thing hasn't finished assimilating the news.

"Whiskey on the way." Giddeon's voice is firm as he gets up and heads inside the house.

"I don't know what to say," Cardan mutters, not addressing anyone in particular.

"We get it, boy," Becca's soft voice cuts through the silence.

"Maybe... I... this... I should think about all this... I don't know..."

Cardan rises from his chair, still looking off-balance. I do the same and take his hand, silently offering my support with a gentle but firm grip.

"Listen, boy," says the Sheriff as he claps Cardan on the shoulder. "Our home's door will always be open to you. When you want to talk, we're here. We are family. Your family."

Cardan nods, not saying a word. I don't know what I would do if I were in his shoes.

I appreciate being here with him.

He throws open the door for me with a ferocity that shows the intensity of his turmoil, and then hastily hustles around the Jeep to join me. As we drove in stony silence, I knew he had no idea where we were going, and yet I am too afraid to speak up.

"If you want, you can drop me off in the orchard, or I can call a ride." My voice came out as a trembling whisper.

Cardan frowned without looking at me, his game face firmly set upon his gaze as he navigated us down the street.

"Elena, I need you with me," he growls. "No, I want you with me, baby. We're going home." With the direction of our destination laid plain before him, he reached over and entwined my fingers in his own. His lips brushed against my skin softly as he continued driving forward.

"I should talk to my mother," Cardan mumbles under his breath as he pulled into an illuminated parking lot behind the shop. Night has already sunk deep into the cityscape, but this place was well lit. From here I could see the entrance clear as day.

"I understand. I'm going to give you some privacy," I reply softly. This is the right thing to do; as a family they both need to deal with this.

But he stops me in a quick move, holding my hand. "Hey, I didn't actually mean it that way. It was just something on my mind," He reveals while opening his door and stepping out into the winter air. "It's freezing out here; let's go inside."

"Are you still going to call your mother?" My question follows him as he quickly punches the code into the lock and opens the door.

"Later," he answers while scooping me up into his arms like a doll and carrying me across the threshold of his apartment. Hanging onto him tightly for dear life.

"But when you said..." Again my words are cut short by his lips on mine, melting away all thoughts except for being safe within his embrace.

"Later..." He breathes against my mouth before walking us further towards the place where hearts are welcomed home.

The moment our lips come together I can feel the sparks flying. Our mouths search hungrily, tongues entangling and exploring each other's depths. We cling to one another, neither wanting it to end for a single second.

"Take off your top. Let me feel you," he growls in my ear, and I oblige quickly, eager to please him. His hands travel around my back, mine twining through his hair as we move closer. His beard scratching against my neck as we dance to an unknown rhythm.

This is so perfect that words fail me. The wood of the ladder imprints its texture onto my skin, but I don't care. All I want is for him to keep going faster and harder.

"I have to slow down, be softer," he groans in agony as though fighting against himself. "But I can't. I can't. You feel too good to not take it further."

My heart slams against my ribcage as I moan his name in a strange voice that doesn't even sound like my own. All the muscles in my body tensing as I reach full intensity, and every inch of me trembles with pleasure.

He follows suit moments later, his body stiffening until it feels like a bowstring ready to launch into oblivion. He lowers his head onto my chest with a guttural groan before finally resting still.

This is what love should feel like -strong and powerful beyond logic or understanding- my story was rewritten, and my fate changed forever by this moment.

And now that we are here, I don't know what comes next...

CHAPTER NINETEEN

"What do you want to do?" I demand of Cardan when we pause for breath after the second round. "Well, I have some ideas," he replies as his piercing green eyes bore into me. He lifts his head and looks at me intently while I remain sprawled beneath him between the pillows. "How about we play just the tip… peach edition? Do you think you can handle it?"

I thump his shoulder with a laugh, but there is an edge to my voice. "You know exactly what I'm talking about, don't even try to avoid the topic."

He shrugs nonchalantly and grins mischievously. His thick brown hair falls messily around his face; he looks utterly irresistible. "You can't blame a guy for trying!"

"Do not try to distract me, mister," I say sternly and raise an eyebrow at him. "I asked you something serious."

His chuckle dies away as he sighs and finally meets my gaze once more. "With you, I always want…" He trails off as he kisses my belly lightly.

"Don't change the subject... be honest with me about how you feel."

Another sigh escapes him before he speaks again, this time softer than before. "I don't know what to make of all these feelings… after hating him for so long, now I understand why he never came back, but I'm overwhelmed by conflicting emotions."

What is the right answer? What should I say to make it better?

"It takes courage to face your past. You need to break away from this and start healing yourself, but it won't be easy. It will take time, and you can't do it alone; find a therapist or someone who can help you."

He stares into my eyes, his expression unreadable as he processes my words.

"Do you speak from experience?" His voice rips open an old wound I thought I had healed, scalding pain radiating through me with every word. Tears blur my vision as the truth of his statement hits me hard. He pulls me close, pressing a gentle kiss against my forehead. "I'm sorry. I was an asshole. These last few days have been hard on us."

More than in his words, in his eyes, there is so much sincerity that it is impossible for me not to believe him.

And forgive him.

"Why don't you take the first step and talk to your mother?"

Cardan turns around, gets out of bed naked, and goes downstairs to find his pants. Since we entered the apartment a couple of hours ago, we left a trail of clothes in our wake.

In the short time we have been together, we have developed trust; he moves naked without giving it the slightest attention. Although with a body like his, I wouldn't feel self-conscious about walking around like God brought me into the world. With the phone pressed to his ear, he sits on the edge of the bed and begins to explain to his mother what happened.

"No, I wasn't alone," he tells his mother. "Elena went with me." Silence while listening to something she says. "Yes. Yes." Silence again. "No, Mom, I'm fine. It isn't necessary to..."

He closes his eyes and rubs them using his thumb and forefinger. He looks emotionally exhausted.

And then more silence.

"Yes, I know. Your only son." He growls. "Okay, woman... yes, we'll see you Monday at the airport."

He drops the phone on the bed and sighs before looking at me.

"My mother," he explains. "She's crazy to meet you."

I give him a smile, although I am dying... I don't know if I'm ready for that moment to come. What if she doesn't like me?

Cardan smiles and comes closer as if he were reading my mind. "She will love you."

"I'm the answer to her prayers, huh?" I scoff to take the weight off the situation.

"And mine," he declares before leaning in to kiss me on the lips.

"Oh yeah?"

"You have no idea how much."

"What if you show me?"

He walks away, smiling at me. But there is something else. This man is hiding something.

"Now, who's the fiend?" he jokes. "But I think the best thing is that we sleep for a while, we have early morning plans."

"Do we?"

"Early." Oh my, that smile. It does things to me.

"How early are we talking?"

"Before the sun rises."

"Have you gone crazy, Malone? It's Sunday, my only day off. And you want me to get out of bed with the sun?"

"Exactly," he replies. "And I promise you it will be worth it."

"I hope you are a man of your word."

"You know it well."

Oh, I do!

♡♡♡

"Where are we going?" I ask him for the umpteenth time.

True to the first part of his promise, Cardan made me get out of bed before six in the morning. Now he's driving the Jeep in the dark, I think we're going north, but I'm not sure.

The first rays of the sun begin to break through the darkness just as Cardan parks the Jeep on a lot that seems empty.

"We're here," he announces.

"Where are we?"

"Surprise," he yells, spreading his arms. A strange noise is heard, and a flame appears.

It isn't empty, after all.

"What is this?"

"Since you want to continue living your adventure but swimming with sharks isn't your thing… let's fly."

There's a big basket, a hot air balloon… and *his smile*.

This time I'm not worried about what might happen. I'm already in free-fall.

I throw myself into his arms without thinking of anything else.

I'm going to fly with him. I'm going to fall with him. I will live for him.

For the two of us.

The decision is made. Tomorrow I'll go see Dax, and as soon as possible, I will start my treatment.

If I have a chance to live, I will reach for it and take it with both hands.

And Cardan will be there to give me his strength when mine fails me.

This is what it feels like.

It's scary. And it is exciting.

"Let's go?" he asks me while his hands caress my back.

At another time, I would die to know everything, from the itinerary to the certification of the instructor to whether we would be given parachutes. Just like I did with the skydiving school. But now, nothing else matters.

Cardan and I head up in a big basket suspended under a hot air balloon. We rise into the star-choked blackness above the tree line. The morning is quite cold, and I appreciate having brought the right clothes. Without Cardan's body heat radiating off of me, it's easy to shiver even in these bulky long johns and parka.

I wrap my arm around his waist; despite the thick layers of fabric that separate us, I've never felt as close to him as I do in this moment. And that's saying something because last night... wow, our most intimate moments were shared among the stars and shadows at midnight on top of a mountain under the solstice moon.

The basket begins its descent, breaking out of flight over Butterfly Meadow as its shadow ripples across it and onto the trees beyond it. As Cardan promised, a special present during my birthday celebration is coming to an end.

The east blushes a deep rose-red with sunrise while the fog gives way before us. This feels good. So peaceful it seems unreal we can move through this cloud and stay aloft by flapping giant pieces of cloth filled with hot air heated by candles shoved into a metal box full of rocks! It smells fresh here—so much better than dirty diesel exhaust fumes or burning trash or potpourri scorched by grease lamps or smoggy air!

A little magic some mornings is just what you need.

In the past, I would have been impatient to learn everything, knowing the itinerary, how long the ride will take, if the instructor was certified, and if he had done this many times before. Just like I did with skydiving school. But now nothing else matters.

Savoring this surprise that Cardan has prepared for me.

Wriggling into the big basket, with excitement swelling in my chest. A brisk chill hangs in the air, yet I'm glad I donned this outfit for the occasion. In this moment, I've never felt closer to him than ever before—not that anyone nearby can tell us apart!

He holds me close as we watch the sunrise in our own little world that just happens to be inside a giant hot air balloon basket surrounded by mist rising off the Sacramento River. The air smells sweet, like pine needles or warm honey, and it cradles me in its softness.

The view shifts as we float toward a cluster of trees on an island across the water and rise above them. This adventure is better than parachuting because it is less scary; it is more serene, but just as exciting. We fly over treetops so close that I can almost touch them, feel their branches brushing my arms and cheek as they pass beneath me.

This is awesome!

"And now a special surprise," announces Jon, the pilot. Yes, believe it or not, those who drive these balloons are called pilots.

Cardan wraps his arms around my waist, effectively trapping me between the basket and his body. As if there was any other place I'd rather be. My knees feel weak, and I lean against him, his warmth feeling good through his coat.

We approach Lake Berryessa and begin our descent. For a moment I get scared; this whole thing feels like a free-fall ride at an amusement park. I decide to let the fear aside, be free of it, that no matter what happens next, it was worth opening my heart to his wonderful man. Jon makes us drop slowly towards the water, it's stunning to see ourselves reflected in the mirror of the water.

I'm ready. I'm going to kick my problems right in the ass.

I turn around to kiss him, to thank him for doing this for me.

And, right at that moment, something doesn't feel right.

My heart pounds in my chest, and my mouth runs dry as foreboding fills me.

"Cardan," I moan, grasping onto the only thing that seems real in this moment. My hands have grown icy cold in the passing seconds and a heavy weight settles over me like a blanket of despair.

"Cardan," I repeat, desperation squeezing my throat tight. But I'm not sure if another sound leaves my lips as the world around me melts into nothingness. Darkness consumes me, until I felt like I was trapped in the depths of an endless abyss.

CHAPTER TWENTY

Cardan

There are those who say that our destiny is written from the moment we are born. Others argue that life offers us options, and we decide which way to go.

I have decided to play a little, to venture. Seek new experiences, take risks, and hope for the best.

When I came to this town to open a new business, I wasn't expecting to find her.

The girl who is looking for an adventure. And I am the man who usually leaves everything to chance.

When I met her, everything changed. Something inside me ignited, and I knew it was time to change destiny. My next bet wasn't just for me. My bet was on both of us.

One moment she's all happy, looking at me bright-eyed, full of joy, and something else I don't dare describe. The next, she falls into my arms like a rag doll.

"We have to go back now!" I yell at Jon, the pilot I met a few days ago when I started planning this. "Elena, baby," I beg her to open her eyes. To say to fuck myself, *something*.

I just want her to wake up.

It seems that fucking time has stopped and that this bloody balloon is moving at a slower and slower pace. I take my phone from my pocket to call 911. Of course, there is no signal up here.

"In ten minutes, we'll be back on the ground," Jon lets me know. Ten minutes is too long.

Elena's breathing becomes slower and slower, and I feel like I'm losing her, like sand between my fingers.

"Baby," I ask, kissing her cheeks, her nose, her lips. "Please wake up, Elena. Look at me."

But it is in vain. Neither does she move nor does she open her eyes.

And I am desperate.

I'm sure all my blood has frozen. And, for the first time in many years, I find myself praying for her to open her eyes and tell me that everything is going to be okay.

What I feel is more than fear. It's panic.

My entire body trembles.

By the time the balloon touches the ground again, I can barely stand. Somehow, I succeed, carrying a still unconscious Elena in my arms to my Jeep.

Just when I'm buckling her up, after accommodating her in the passenger seat, she wakes up. Words aren't enough to describe my relief. I almost get down on my knees to thank God, and at the same time, I want to fill her face with kisses.

"Cardan…" she whispers in a voice I barely recognize as hers.

What the fuck is going on?

"Easy, baby, we're going to get help."

My foot slams on the accelerator, pushing my car to its limits as I race toward Sunny Hills General. Streetlights come and go like blurs of red and orange as I fight against what it looks like a sea of cars that have suddenly sprouted like weeds from the ground below.

Every passing second is torture as my fingers drum on the steering wheel in a mix of rage and fear, counting down the minutes until we reach the hospital. At last, it appears like a shimmering beacon in the distance, but nothing can get rid of this feeling of dread in my stomach. When I reach the entrance, I don't bother turning off the engine or locking up the Jeep before racing into the hospital with Elena in my arms.

Inside, nurses scurry around us as they take her away on a stretcher. Alone, I am left standing in the hall, unable to help or protect her anymore. As she disappears through those doors, it feels like part of me has gone with her—leaving me here with only an empty hollow feeling inside.

"Information about Elena Posada?" I ask the nurse behind the glass at the reception for the umpteenth time. I'm ready to fight my way to her, but in a moment, they would call the police, and Elena needs me here.

"Are you family?" the woman asks.

Her boyfriend? I've always hated that damn word. It's too childish.

Her lover? That is not enough to describe how I feel about her.

She's mine, that's what I want to say. Instead, the realization hits me hard. "Shit. Her father," I remind myself. "Her father needs to know we are here."

No one answers at home, so after thinking about what to do, I decide to call Destinee. She works here, after all. And she'll surely help me get some information.

"I hope you're inviting us back to Napa. I just ended my shift." She greets me with a joke, but now isn't the moment for that.

"Destinee, this is important," I say. "I'm at the hospital with Elena, she fainted a while ago, while the balloon ride."

Through the line, I can hear her gasping. "What? Elena is where?" she asks, worry filling her voice.

"I need you to come here right now; nobody here wants to tell me anything. And please give Mr. Posada a call."

"I'm coming."

Mr. Posada enters the waiting room before Destinee does. The man looks distressed, which is normal, but not surprised somehow.

"I'm waiting for news…" I say while standing, offering him my hand.

"When I was on my way here, I spoke with Dax Pearson, a family doctor friend. He must be with her right now, we will have news soon."

"I'm so sorry, Mr. Posada. As you know, we met at the skydiving school, I have no idea Elena would…" Suddenly, I feel like an anxious child in front of his father, ready for penance.

"Call me, Ignacio, this mister shit is getting old."

Mr. Posada flops into the chair next to me. For a few moments, neither of us says anything, when I am about to ask him how he's so calm, I see the clear signs of fatigue on his face.

"Have you ever wondered why I welcomed you so openly in my home? Why I encourage your relationship with my daughter?"

What he says is true, but the bottom line is I still don't understand.

A lump forms in my throat, stopping me from answering.

"Although it is difficult for me to accept it as a father, Elena isn't a girl anymore. She's an adult, and she should be the one to talk to you. But as a parent I ask you to be here to listen to what she has to say. I'm trusting that what you told me that day at home is true. It's time to prove it."

I look at the man's face. His skin looks pale, despite being tanned by the sun. There's something here, something bigger than the two of us. And I don't mean the love we both feel for Elena.

It's something more.

"You're a man, Cardan, not a child." Mr. Posada—Ignacio, I remind myself—rises from his chair, patting me on the shoulder. "Now I'm going to find Dax. It's time someone gave me information about my daughter."

After what happened yesterday and even in this shitty situation, I feel grateful for the acceptance of this man who loves his family fiercely and knows the pain of losing the other half of his heart firsthand.

About two hours have passed when a man about my age appears wearing jeans and a plaid flannel shirt.

"Dax," Ignacio greets him.

"I'm sorry it took so long; these things take time," he explains. "Elena is stable, right now they are getting her settled in a room. We'll take advantage of the fact that she is here to carry out some tests. The arrhythmia she suffered caused her to faint, given her condition and without treatment…"

Her condition? What in the living hell is he talking about?

"Is she going to be, okay?" Elena's father cuts him off. I would have to be foolish not to realize that the question was to cut off the doctor's explanation. "When can I see her?"

"I would like to speak with you privately, sir. You see, Elena…"

Mr. Posada puts a hand on Dax's shoulder and leads him to a corner. I look at them, trying to guess what the fuck they're hiding. What's happening with my girl?

Elena is going to be fine. She's going to get out of here on her own two feet. And then she and I are going to have a long conversation.

♡♡♡

"Room B-432," I repeat the information that appears on the screen in the waiting room. I'm ready to face whatever comes my way.

This has been a very long day, and it isn't even dark yet. Somehow, I'm not tired. It's something else. My mind is racing a thousand miles per hour. And it's not going to rest until I see Elena wide-eyed, blaming me for a change. Or talking nonstop about her methods for dehydrating mangoes or the perfect mix of chili peppers for seasoning.

My phone rings in my pocket. I pick it up to see my mother's name appear on the screen. Mr. Posada walks ahead of me while I stay in the hall to take the call.

"Mom," I greet her. "I'll call you in a bit. I'm at the hospital…"

I hear her gasp. "Are you ok? What happened?"

"It isn't me. It's Elena?" I hear her chocking, after that she plagues me with questions.

I don't know how to answer. I really have no idea how I feel. And from Elena, well, everything feels like I'm floating in limbo.

"At this moment, I was about to go in to see her, I'll call you in a bit."

"But, son, the thing is…"

I must hasten this conversation. My body cries out to see her, to know that she is okay.

"I'll call you later." I hear my mother protest, but without giving her a chance, I press the red button. I'll make it up to her later. I'm sure she'll understand when I explain what happened and she meets Elena.

I walk to the door, which is open. However, the privacy curtain is drawn. Elena's father's words stop me in my tracks.

"You have to tell him," he says.

"Tell him what? That I am going to die? That I am the girl who has no future?"

The earth quakes under my feet, the ground yawning wide as if to swallow me whole. My stomach lurches like I'm on a rollercoaster ride to hell. What does it all mean?

"What the fuck are you talking about?" I ask her, moving the curtain aside.

"Cardan," she replies, and tears come to her eyes. But the answers I need elude me, mocking me with their absence.

"What the fuck is your father talking about, Elena?" She needs to start talking *now*.

She stares out the window, tears streaming down her face like a raging river. My heart shatters into a million pieces as I watch her, and I want to sprint to her side and wrap her in my arms and tell her how much she means to me. I will shield her with my body and kiss away her fears until she believes me that all will be alright. That no problem is too big for us to solve.

"Elena?" her father and I say in unison. Although in a different tone.

"I have the same disease that killed my mother," she whispers in a shaky voice.

My heart jumps out of my chest as if a giant wrecking ball had collided with it, stealing away the air I desperately needed in order to survive.

"Hypertrophic cardiomyopathy," she carries on emotionlessly. "That is the reason why I started this journey. That is why I live day by day because planning beyond that isn't an option. Because death is knocking at my door, and I can't hide from it forever."

The rage inside me increases with every passing second, and before I know it, I hear myself snarling "That's not true" with the force of lightning.

I refuse to accept her fate and so I will fight for her until my last breath, no matter what happens or how much time passes.

"It is," she snaps at me, finally looking into my eyes for the first time. "So save yourself the trouble, Cardan. This is over."

A fire lights up in my veins, and I reply with fierce determination: "The fuck we are!" before storming out of the room.

If she needs space, then I will give her just that. If she needs time, she shall have it. Then, she needs to be ready. She must be prepared for I will never surrender. A plan of attack is essential for victory: fall back before attacking; think carefully about every step taken forward—those are the main rules of war, and that's exactly, what I'm going to do.

♡♡♡

The Jeep feels as if it is in a vice, crushing, suffocating me. I need to drown my sorrows. Harder and harder I press the pedal, until I finally arrive at home, where I find what I am looking for: a bottle of tequila. The irony stings.

"Viva Mexico," I jeer, raising the bottle to my lips and taking a big gulp. Again and again, I take swigs from the cold glass as my thoughts come crashing down like waves around me. Elena's warning about the impending doom that awaits me echoes in my mind.

No! I refuse to give up without a fight—this can't be it.

But before I can even process my feelings further, a hard knock on the door shakes me out of my reverie. Insistent. Panic washes over me—who could be here? I'm more drunk than I thought, with no strength left to stand up. Another loud bang on the door and fear turns into anger—I'm not done yet! With renewed energy, I stumble to the door and wrench it open...

The floor is against me. The bastard insists on swaying when I try to get up.

I rest my arm on the wall and try again, this time with better results.

The person outside seems to be in a hurry to come and bother me because he seems to want to knock down the door.

"I'm coming," I bellow, trying to calm the deafening clamor.

I twist the lock while someone crashes against the wooden door, almost knocking me over. Five foot five of pure sassiness and tenacity storms into my home for the first time.

"What do you want?" It was the only thing that could escape my foggy mind.

"If you had let me explain, you would have known by now," she replied curtly.

"I'm working on something," I reply acidly, that's true. Kinda.

"Oh, I see," she accepts acridly. "Brewing moonshine no doubt."

"Just tell me why you're here," I demand of her, eager to be done with her so I can go back to what I was doing. My head is starting to ache.

"You may be grown up Cardan Joseph, but that doesn't mean you get to talk like that to your mother."

CHAPTER TWENTY-ONE

Elena

My father looms in the chair at the side of my bed, his eyes burning into me without uttering a single word. His gaze takes up the whole room, and it speaks for him—a warning, a judgment, but most of all an accusation. I haven't shed a tear since Cardan ran away hours ago, and I'm not sure whether to feel proud or heartbroken. Is it good that my heart feels like it's been torn apart, yet my soul survives?

"The next time you plan a visit to the hospital, just make sure to keep your scheduled appointment," Dax says as he enters my room. "There is no need to cause all this fuss. Much less on a Sunday."

"You have my permission to keep her here for as long as it takes to run all the tests and start treatment," my father announces. "Make it like rehab."

If I was in the mood, those words would make me roll my eyes.

"I had already decided to accept all of this anyway." I don't have to explain what I mean by all. They both know what I'm talking about.

"And when did that wonderful revelation happen?" my father asks.

I look at Dax, who pretends to study the chart with my vital signs with renewed attention.

"This morning, just when we were on the balloon."

"I think it's time to stop all that nonsense, *niña*..."

"This time, it wasn't my idea, blame Cardan."

Cardan. My chest hurts when I remember him. Thinking about what could have been...

Thinking about 'what could have been' is pointless. It doesn't matter, or does it?

"Well," Dax cuts the thread of our conversation. "While you're here, we are going to start giving you some IV medications. I want to see how you react to the treatment. As soon as I have the results of your test, I will talk to my friend, who's a specialist in hypertrophic cardiomyopathy. I would like you to get the best possible care as well as the most up-to-date treatment."

Mentally I am already doing the math. "Does my insurance cover all that?" And then, if there is any copay, I'd be broke in no time.

My father clears his throat before speaking. "Money is no problem, Dax. My sons and I agree, whatever Elena needs..."

I open and close my mouth, gaping like a fish. "When did you and my brothers have this conversation?"

"The other day at the house," he answers, smiling. "And a little while ago on the phone, when I let them know that we're here."

This is what means to be part of a tight family like mine. For better or worse.

"Which means the Posada men are plotting against me..." That's not a question. It is a fact.

"And the five of us agree that if we have to tie you up to keep you in the hospital and get you treatment..."

"We already talked about that not going to be necessary," I reply. "Dax, what is the next step?"

"On the ultrasound, we saw that the walls of your heart have started to thicken," he begins to explain. That is what the disease is about, the walls of the heart thicken, preventing blood from circulating through the ventricles and atria, as it would in a healthy organ. "However, at this point, I don't think surgery is necessary just yet. My prognosis is that you will respond well to the treatment."

"And episodes like today?" I ask. Wishing to know what my limits are.

"As long as you follow all the recommendations, you will be able to lead a relatively normal life, Elena. Science makes leaps and bounds every day; life expectancy has increased a lot. Let's have a little faith once in a while. It doesn't hurt anyone, right? "

"You." A voice booms from the door.

There's Cardan, tall and imposing as ever. His hair is a little damp, like he just got out of the shower, wearing jeans and a long-sleeved grey Henley. He looks drop dead gorgeous.

But what is he doing here?

"Me?" I ask him. He started this game.

"Do you want to live an adventure?" He comes closer to me.

My jaw is open. My father and Dax look between us, their eyes, full of amusement.

"Depends on what adventure it is, Malone," I reply. "Swimming with sharks is definitely off the list, and I don't think my doctor would recommend a mission to the International Space Station under these circumstances."

He laughs, so much so that he throws his head back. I love every second the sound lasts.

"Your adventure is to live with me, fight with me," he announces as he sits on the bed next to me. His big hands, framing my face. "Love me. I dare you. Love me, and let me love you, Elena. I know you think your heart is broken, so here

I am—putting mine in your hands. If you lack strength, take mine. I'm strong enough; take all my strength if you need it. But I need you to promise me something."

I look into those green eyes that have hypnotized me from the first time I saw them.

"Open your wings and fly, baby. I'll be here to catch you."

That makes me smile, remembering the day at the skydiving school.

"Do you think you are in a position to be demanding?"

He smiles sideways. God, the things that mouth does to me. But I shouldn't forget that we are in a hospital. With my father and my physician in the room.

"I want all of you, Elena. And I'm going to give you all of me and then some. Forget about living one day at a time. Our forever waits for us. This is our destiny, baby."

"I think I can bear it," I reply.

Our lips touch, and the magic sparks again.

"I'm so in love with you," he says just after our lips touch.

"Good, because I love you too, Malone."

How wrong I've been all this time. My heart isn't broken. Just walking at a different pace, and it's time I learn to live with it.

And no, we aren't going to live happily ever after. There will be fights. And tears. But there will also be kissing and making up.

After all, life is an adventure, right?

CHAPTER TWENTY-TWO

Cardan

Ever since I received the news about Elena's deteriorating condition, I've been on a mission to make her life feel worth living. While battling my own demons, I stumbled upon Sunny Hills and found myself in a situation where I didn't want to leave. And then, as if by fate, I found her. Elena was like a beacon of light in my otherwise bleak existence. She has decided to fight, and I'm determined to be right by her side through it all.

I spared no expense in getting her the best possible medical attention money could buy—flying in a world-renowned surgeon from Stanford and ensuring that she has everything she needs for a successful surgery. And when it comes to making her mine, well, let's just say that I have some very big plans—including slipping a big ass diamond on her finger after this is over.

As we sit here in the hospital waiting room, there's a palpable sense of tension in the air. Elena's brothers and sister-in-law are sitting in the private waiting room while her father tries his best to remain stoic. My mother is here too—she loves Elena almost as a daughter. And watching the two women of my life interact provides me with infinite joy. Mom always wanted a daughter, and for Elena, having a motherly figure around is heartwarming.

In another corner of the room, Destinee and Ignacio are deep in conversation with Dax, the cardiologist, another reminder of how interconnected our lives have become since we first crossed paths. It's hard not to think about how different things would be if we'd never met.

But now is not the time for regrets or what-ifs, we're here for Elena and nothing else matters.

And so, we wait. The helicopter I fleeted to carry the surgeon should be landing any minute now, and once she arrives, it'll be go-time.

I steal a glance at Elena across the room—she's pacing back and forth, wringing her hands anxiously. My heart goes out to her, and I vow once again to be by her side no matter what.

"What if I shit myself during the surgery?" She blurts from nowhere.

"I think that happens during labor, not a heart surgery."

"What?" She screeches in horror. Yes, I've been reading a lot. The good, the beautiful, and the worst. I want to have kids with my wonderful woman, and a man like me likes to make plans. "Cardan?"

"It doesn't matter, *bonita*. Doctors have their way to avoid disasters."

Her hands fly to her pajama covered tummy, stroking it as if a baby were nestling there. I'm mesmerized conjuring those images in my mind.

"If that's true, we won't have kids. Ever."

Yes, she has been thinking about it, too.

A smile turns my lips up.

"Don't look at me that way, Malone!" She scolds me, pointing with her finger. "I'm serious."

No, she's not, plus, I have my ways. I can't wait to discuss this subject tangled in the sheets of our bed. Hard and deeply.

"Doctor Fleming is here," Destinee cuts our conversation. Her face a mix of hope and concern for the girl who has been her best friend for years. "She will be here in a few minutes. Dax is updating her right now."

"There is no time for me to run, right?" The tension hangs in the air like a thick fog, as Elena starts her pacing again. I step forward and take her into my arms, letting her know that our future awaits us. Her body trembles and I feel helpless to do anything but hold her tightly. "You're brave and strong," I whisper into her ear, wishing desperately for any words that will soothe the fear in her heart.

"Even a broken heart can beat again, eh?" She murmurs back with a hint of hope.

"Always." My voice is strong, filled with determination.

"And you promised me a celebration." She says softly, nuzzling against my chest.

"You'll get it," I tell her, rocking my hips gently as I joke and not joke at the same time.

We won't deny the obvious attraction between us, and she giggles against me before Doctor Fleming interrupts the moment.

There's no more time for small talk; Elena must prepare for surgery, no matter how much fear grips our hearts. Ignacio, Dax, and Destinee join us, all fighting their own battles of concern for Elena.

The doctor announces she must go ready herself, and Elena crumbles into sobs while clinging into her father embrace.

"I'll be here waiting for you, *Bonita*," I tell her firmly, pushing away the thought of giving my life if it meant saving hers.

Elena Posada is my world—my woman, my future... My fated.

EPILOGUE

Elena

Two and a half years later

These are the longest three minutes in the history of humankind.

I swear I'm sweating bullets. When did our bathroom become so small? I'm suffocating in here.

Why can't these things be insta-quick instead of three fucking minutes?

And while I wait for the answer, my mind drifts to the path that brought me to this moment.

Cardan set his mind on a goal. To make me live without fear. Without limits.

And without regrets.

He proposed the weekend after I was released from the hospital. Cardan got on one knee in front of both our families, with the perfect ring, a diamond solitary in a platinum band. The moment was magical, the two of us surrounded by unconditional love and support.

After that, we started planning. However, we both had different ideas about how we wanted our big day to be. I wanted to elope; Cardan wanted a ceremony with all our loved ones around us.

For me, the party and all the fuss weren't necessary, just the fact that this beautiful man was mine.

Cardan wanted to make it big.

"I couldn't care less about the dress nor the party," I said one night after making love. We were living provisionally in his apartment over the garage. His hands were wandering on my naked back, and those beautiful green eyes were looking at me intently.

"But I do," he replied. "I want to kiss my wife for the first time in front of our families." Then he smiled, and something inside me melted. I had no power to deny him anything' after growing up just with his mother, Cardan embraced my family and the Malones with gusto. "And I want to undress you afterward and cherish you like the gift of a lifetime that you are."

After those words, I lost the power to say no.

My mother-in-law was a godsend. She helped me to plan every single detail of the wedding. We celebrated our small affair in one of the most beautiful vineyards in Napa.

So, we compromised and splurged a little. I stuffed Cardan in a tuxedo while I walked down the aisle wearing my mother's wedding dress.

Destinee and I found it in a trunk, carefully wrapped in blue tissue paper. The simple design made in delicate ivory silk was classy and very feminine. And to my surprise, it fit me almost perfectly. That morning, I cried a lot on Dee's shoulder after deciding to wear it.

It was a surprise for my father and brothers too. It was a very emotional moment when they saw me for the first time, but it made it more special. She was there with us.

I completed the attire wearing a long hand-embroidered veil, but it wasn't covering my face. It was my biggest wish to see it all including Cardan's misted-eyed while I walked down the aisle. My father and I were walking slow, but my feet wanted to fly. Inside my chest, my heart was beating hard.

At the altar, my man waited for me. And he wasn't alone. Griffin Malone was Cardan's best man. They have developed a close relationship, and his uncle Robert often remarks on how grateful he is that all his boys are married men now. The Sunny Hills female population is safe from the Malone boys, as is his sanity. Four Malone boys are too much—and too hot—to handle.

On days like today, I can't help but be afraid. Life is so fragile. My heart is still broken, but with every single beat, I've chosen to love him. Every day I wake up with a smile on my lips and a hot bearded man beside me.

I love him. Not a single day have I regretted choosing him and this adventure. We've fought, as we both have strong personalities, but also, we quickly make up, often between the sheets of our bed. Cardan built a beautiful home for me in my favorite place here in the orchard. Overlooking the water and my beloved mango trees.

"What are you doing in there?" I hear him say through the closed door.

"What are *you* doing here, Cardan?" I reply, keeping a secret these days is an impossible mission. "Weren't you playing golf with Griffin?"

I can't look at the white stick with him on the other side of the door. I'm losing this battle.

I close my eyes and fake wash my hands. This buys me a couple of minutes until he knocks again.

Impatient as ever…

"Elena, open the door."

"Cardan, I'm able to pee alone." We wrote our own vows, and I never promised to obey my husband. I'm the same spunky girl I have always been. "Let me be!"

A growl fills the silence.

"You washed your hands already," he rebukes. He's not giving me even a minute to draft a plan. "Open the door, *bonita.*"

He knocks again and again.

This is impossible.

I check myself in the mirror. I look horrible, a little greenish, and my hair is a bird's nest. He said he married me for better or worse. *Right?*

"Why are you hiding in there?" he asks. I assume Cardan crosses his arms over his hard chest, which isn't fair since he knows I'm incapable of resisting his big tools.

"Things," that's my short reply as I swing open the door. "What are you doing here? Why did you come back so soon?"

My husband takes my face between his hands. Those green eyes are looking for answers inside me. He knows me too well, and when he's looking at me this way, I'm incapable to lying or hiding something.

"I was worried. You aren't eating well, and yesterday I found you napping at ten in the morning."

Yup, shame on me. Yesterday I went on a walk with my father around the orchard. After that, I was done. We finished the harvest last week; this year went wonderfully. We reached our goal, and I have saved a good amount of fruit to dehydrate.

My little business is booming too. We are now selling in a regional supermarket branch since last season. For that reason, we had to renovate one of our barns to make space for my new machinery and hire three girls to help me with the work. Running two successful businesses isn't an easy task. It's challenging—and frustrating sometimes—but it makes me feel so fulfilled and proud. And the man of my life is always there to support me.

And yes, I haven't felt that well the last few days. I'm tired and moody. At first, I thought an unexpected visit to Dax's office was on the horizon. Then, Aunt Flo didn't come for her monthly visit. Hence, here I am... shaking and queasy, thinking of the right way to tell my husband that we will probably have some company soon.

"You know Dax is just a call away," he whispers while caressing my face softly. Cardan only knows how to love fiercely, with all his heart. And he is teaching me to do it without fears. I know a dark angel is lurking in the shadows. However, I'm learning to take it one day at a time and just hope for the better.

"I guess we will need to call him soon and maybe look for another doctor too..." Gosh, this is hard.

"Why wait? Let's go to the ER right now, baby."

The alarm shadowing in his eyes makes me smile. I touch his chest, my favorite place in the entire world. My hand feeling the steady rhythm of his heart. This is the tune of my life.

"Cardan, look at the vanity," I whisper.

"Why?" His eyes are still focused on mine. He won't budge that easy.

"Look at the vanity, babe."

At my insistence, he does as I tell him, and then I feel him trembling. Yep, he's feeling it too.

Boom.

Boom.

Boom.

"Bonita…"

Here is my answer. The ground is shaking. Our lives are about to change forever.

Cardan takes the test in his hands to look at it closely. As if the damn thing were a mystery.

"How did this happen?"

A smile pulls up my lips, he's more shocked than me.

"Remember when you convinced me about trashing my pills? Well, they were quite effective, and after all the things you like doing to me…"

Keeping the test in his hands, he turns to me to crush me to his chest. I don't know how any air reaches my lungs because Cardan leaves little space for anything else but his love.

"Be careful. You're squishing us!" I fake scold him, but I'm still smiling.

"Do you have any idea how happy I am right now?"

My smile grows. His eyes are shining like never before. That glow says to me more than his words.

"Good to know, Malone. Because I'm shaking and I need you. My mind is reeling…"

He gives me another hug, softer this time. "Don't you worry. I'm not going anywhere. Love, this is…"

There is too much to worry about. Not just my health but the baby. Will it inherit the same condition as I did? There is too much at stake. But I set all my fears aside and enjoy the moment with my husband.

I'm not alone. The man I chose to love is right here with me.

There is a little part of him growing inside me. This is truly a miracle. One we created together with love.

And we'll have a new companion to share this new adventure with. Our big, rambunctious families to lean on when we need it.

Cardan didn't run when the situation turned dark.

He stayed with me, fighting for us. I don't need to be strong all the time, I know he's here with me to put the pieces together again.

This is love. This is life.

And I've learned. Destiny is written in the stars, but fate is something you choose. And I chose to thrive with my own hero. He doesn't need a cape, but his strength makes my heart beat every day.

Yes, I found Cardan Malone, my fated.

THE END

Thank you for reading Fated. I hope you enjoyed the story, craving more of Cardan and Elena? Click here to read an extra hot chapter.

Yes, we are going to Hawaii for their honeymoon!

→ https://dl.bookfunnel.com/7w9bljlqs8

ACKNOWLEDGEMENTS

Oh my, this adventure had been amazing!

I want to start by thanking God for blessing me and for giving me inspiration.

To my daughter who is always there when I need her the most. My wonderful B, thank you for your support, unconditional love and, above all, patience. I love you with all my heart.

To my family, without them I would not be doing this, they have always been my inspiration.

To my Matty Gilbert, thank you for accepting being the perfect image for Cardan.

To Laura, you are a blessing in my life. To Elma and Fer, unconditional love, always. ♥

To Alexia and Dani, I don't know where I'd be without you. I love you, girls!!

To my friends, because they are the best cheerleaders! Thanks for the extra strength, the prayers, the laughter, the patience, and the unconditional support.

To my author friends, thank you so much for being my tribe.

To all the bloggers and instabloggers, for their support and for giving the opportunity to showcase my work. ***THANK YOU!***

Thanks y'all for supporting me with your sweet messages, I can't put into words how much that means to me.

Thank you for reading and support this job I love so much, means the world to me.

From the bottom of my heart... Thank you!

S x

Thank you for reading **FATED.**

I'd love to know your opinion.

It only takes less than a minute and it supports the job I love.

Every review helps.

Sending you all my love ☺

S x

Join my reader's group and stay tunned with all the news and fun!

Susana Mohel's Lollipop Gang

ABOUT THE AUTHOR

Susana Mohel is a *USA Today* best-selling author whose stories sizzle like the sunshine in her Southern California mountains.

Her fast-paced, angsty contemporary romance novels transport readers to a world of spunky heroines and hunky heroes who find their way to a happily ever after... with plenty of spiced-up moments along the way.

When she's not writing, Susana can be found wandering the trails along with her husband or creating chaos in her garden.

BOOKS BY SUSANA MOHEL

Read free with Kindle Unlimited

https://www.susanamohel.com

Want more of the Posada siblings?

Destined _ Martin & Destinee

(Forbidden Standalone Romance)

Wrecked - David & Ella

(Billionaire - Surprise baby romance)

Whispers of My Skin

(Second-Chance/Western Standalone Romance)

Rainstorm

(A Second-Chance, Standalone Romance)

Blank Spaces

(Enemies-to-Lovers Standalone Romance)

Off Limits

(Forbidden/Military Standalone Romance)

Blurred Lines

(Enemies-to-lovers/Reverse-Age-Gape Standalone Romance)

Beyond our Forever

(Second-Chance Standalone Romance)

Unexpected Savior – A Cocky Hero Club Novel

(Second Chance Standalone Romance)

Uncovering Hope – An Office Romance

Big Bad Wolfe – A Red Riding Hood Retelling